PRAISE FOR *SANTA OVERBOARD*

"A fast-paced, enjoyable holiday read that incorporates some of Occoquan's cherished traditions."

—Earnie Porta, PhD, Mayor, Town of Occoquan

"Carolyn McBride's *Santa Overboard* is a delightful continuation of the Potomac Shores series. The way she weaves history and culture in her novels makes her books so special. The holiday spirit of the small town is reminiscent of a great holiday movie. I wish I could live in Potomac Shores and be a member of the Beach Bonfire Babes!"

—Colie Reads

"*Santa Overboard* is a heartwarming romance for the holiday season. Author Carolyn McBride has written a feel-good yarn that embodies the Christmas spirit and is perfect for a cozy read during the holidays. All in all, this is a wholesome book that is bound to raise everyone's spirits. Don't miss out!"

—Readers' Favorite 5-star review

"True to what made *The Cicada Spring* a reader favorite, McBride delivers a charming book full of realistic relationships with a little humor and mystery woven in. Peppered with facts about the region and beautiful imagery of the town, *Santa Overboard* will leave you wanting to plan your own visit to Occoquan this holiday season – 5 out of 5 stars!"

—Read With Lindsey

"Grab a cozy blanket and your favorite Christmas scented candle because we're back with Katie and the Beach Bonfire Babes! This was just the book to get me into the spirit of Christmas plus lots of laughs along the way."

—Simply Nicole

PRAISE FOR *THE CICADA SPRING* AND CAROLYN McBRIDE

"A well-written and absorbing story of resilience that also wonderfully explores and captures the natural beauty of the Occoquan River and its surroundings."

—*Earnie Porta, PhD, Mayor, Town of Occoquan*

"McBride's assured debut launches her Potomac Shores series with a turbulent but uplifting romance . . . , ultimately positing that the only way to navigate rough waters is by taking the helm."

—*BookLife Reviews Editor's Pick*

"McBride sets a vivid scene, and her storytelling consistently engages. An involving tale that balances struggle, love, and hope."

—*Kirkus Reviews*

"Carolyn McBride brings us soulful women's fiction in *The Cicada Spring*. Filled with amazing little bits of insight, you will be hard-pressed not to dig a little deeper into your own life to find that which 'feeds your soul.' *The Cicada Spring* is a must-read!"

—*Readers' Favorite 5-star review*

"*The Cicada Spring* is women's fiction at its best. I have no hesitation in awarding it five stars and recommending it to anyone who loves great women's fiction or just appreciates a talented wordsmith and storyteller." —*Reedsy Discovery 5-star review*

"Have you watched *Sullivan's Crossing* or *Virgin River*? Carolyn McBride's *The Cicada Spring* gave me the same vibes! I found these characters to be incredibly relatable, like I could meet them while grocery shopping and pick up a quick chat and just hit it off."

—*Simply Nicole*

SANTA OVERBOARD

A Potomac Shores Holiday

CAROLYN McBRIDE

MAKE WAVES
—PRESS—

www.makewavespress.com

Publisher's Cataloging-in-Publication data
Names: McBride, Carolyn, author.
Title: Santa overboard: A Potomac Shores holiday / Carolyn McBride.
Series: Potomac Shores
Description: Hypoluxo, FL: Make Waves Press, 2024.
Identifiers: LCCN: 2024915857
ISBN: 979-8-9902958-2-7 (paperback) | 979-8-9902958-3-4 (ebook)
Subjects: LCSH Christmas--Fiction. | Virginia--Fiction. | Chesapeake Bay Region (Md. and Va.)--Fiction. | Potomac River Valley--Fiction. | Family--Fiction. | Friendship--Fiction. | Middle-aged women--Fiction. | Romance fiction. | BISAC FICTION / Romance / Holiday | FICTION / Romance / Romantic Comedy | FICTION / Family Life / Marriage & Divorce | FICTION / Romance / Contemporary Classification: LCC PS3613.C37 S36 2024 | DDC 813.6--dc23

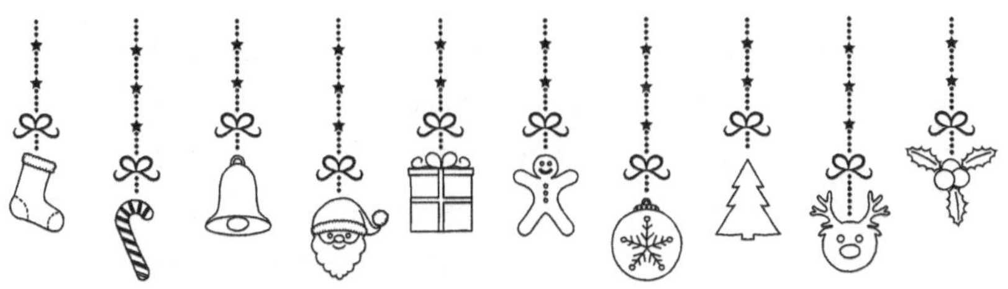

PROLOGUE

Holiday traditions today blend the ancient and sacred, modern and commercial. Some customs remain relatively true to form, like the lighting of the Christian Advent wreath during the Christmas season and the Jewish menorah during Hanukkah. Then there are the odd pagan legends, like the story of Odin the Wanderer and his Nordic eight-legged horse, which morphed into our mainstream Santa Claus and his eight reindeer. Rudolph came much later, created for a coloring book distributed by the Montgomery Ward department store in 1939.

Yet in a world where a green monster steals Christmas presents from Whoville and an Elf on the Shelf secretly moves around the house, there is nary a mention of the creepy, crawly yuletide spider and the cobwebs of Christmas past. Instead, the stealthy arachnid is left to adorn haunted houses every Halloween, a fate unbefitting its benevolent history in Eastern European legend.

According to Ukrainian folklore, a poor widow was unable

to provide presents for her children at Christmas. She didn't even have the means to decorate the tree that had taken root in the dirt floor of their meager hut. On Christmas Eve, an industrious spider spun strands of webbing around the branches. In the morning light, the tree glistened in gold and silver, and from that day forward, the poor family was blessed with riches.

While tinsel has fallen out of favor for environmental reasons, the inspiration for it may be that lowly spider, one of nature's master architects, who brought a little Christmas magic to a family in need. Today, Ukrainians hang "pavuchkys," or little spiders, on their Christmas trees for prosperity in the year ahead, and in some Eastern European countries, it's considered good luck to find a spider or a spider's nest in the tree.

Whether we realize we need it or not, we can all use a little holiday magic to help us change our perspective and see the lives we've architected for ourselves in a different light. The intricately woven strands of our lives are rarely obvious, but in the right light, they envelope us in a delicate honeycomb of interconnected moments, weaving a web of memories as bright as Rudolph's red nose or the red berries on a holly tree in winter.

～ x ～

CHAPTER 1

MOVEMBER

"**A**hoy, my land lassy! Ready for a moonlight serenade?"
A deep and amusingly fake Scottish accent interrupted Katie's thoughts as the *Sea Bug* emerged from the twilight and drifted toward shore, the white hull of the Potomac Science Center's boat taking on the lavender hue of the fading light. The tall man at the helm wore his trademark red hat, and he grinned from ear to ear as he held up a guitar in one hand and a bottle of wine in the other.

He looks like a teenage boy pulling out all the stops.

At fifty-one, Katie never thought she would feel sixteen again, but her "marsh man"—a former marine scientist turned behavioral archaeologist—had a way of making every kiss feel like the first. Better than the first. The best. With his sandy towhead, he resembled a grown-up Dennis the Menace. And his arresting hazel eyes changed like the colors of the river, some days more muddy, other times a deep greenish blue with specks of gold.

She couldn't help but smile at the nicknames they'd given each other. Her "marsh man" would have to change his tune when her new boat arrived, but for a few more days, she was still landlocked, and he enjoyed reminding her of that. "Land lassy" had a nice ring to it. Both in their fifties, they felt they were too old to call each other boyfriend and girlfriend.

Dr. Deke Kinnebrook had been a mainstay in her life for the past nine months. She had known him even longer, ever since she had inherited the river house in Virginia and moved back from South Florida at the beginning of the global pandemic. She had lost her mother to COVID, and the losses had continued to accumulate during lockdown, from her hard-earned job and "dream" marriage to her family's beloved boat, the *Potomac Princess*.

Focus on the gain.

At the same time, with Thanksgiving only a week away, Katie knew she had so much to be thankful for after the past two years. She would normally lament the winter ahead, but with the world reopening again, she looked forward to a memorable, pull-out-all-the-stops kind of holiday season before her daughter went back to college and her younger brother married his fiancée. Since both of her parents had passed away and Belle and Ben were establishing distinct lives of their own—her brother's on the other side of the world in India—the holidays would never be the same again.

In rebuilding her life on the banks of the Potomac, she had leaned on her group of besties, the Beach Bonfire Babes, and together their shop in the nearby town of Occoquan was keeping them afloat, financially to some extent but more so in stimulating creativity and re-envisioning their lives after

COVID. Replacing her mother's travel agency with a gathering place for artists of all sorts was the perfect solution at a time when most people longed for community again. The tabletop s'mores stations in Bonfire Voices were a huge hit and always reminded Katie of where her bonds with most of the women had formed, as girls on her parents' beach sharing dreams around a real bonfire.

And ever so slowly she had allowed herself to lean on Deke, taking baby steps toward a life with him. She wanted their first Christmas together to be extra special, and she wouldn't mind some frolicking under the mistletoe too. Maybe they were finally ready for more.

"You're late!" Katie shouted, startling the nearby geese who honked loudly in seeming annoyance. "I was beginning to worry my marsh man ran aground on the way over here."

"Nah, the tide is super high tonight with the full moon. I had to run back to Occoquan to feed and walk Brigid."

"Aww, you could have brought her to the house to play with Darwin. You know that," Katie said.

Her Old English sheepdog and his boxer had become fast friends. Although they weren't water dogs by breed, they certainly enjoyed their share of boat rides.

"Well, normally I would rely on Danylo to take her out, but he's teaching a class tonight. Plus, he says he needs to prep for his presentation at the gallery. He's kinda nervous about speaking in front of strangers. He'd much rather be behind a paint can and up on a scaffold."

Deke's roommate was a world-renowned graffiti artist from Ukraine who had been commissioned to spray-paint a wildlife mural on the side of the science center after competing in a global contest sponsored by the center's affiliated university. Bonfire Voices was hosting a meet-the-artist night for Danylo as part of the town's upcoming HolidayFest for artisans.

Katie waded out to the boat in giant white rubber boots, hoping the cold water wouldn't seep over the edges into her knee-length wool socks. She missed being at the helm as much as she missed her floating dock, another victim of the massive river of mud that had cut through her land, defining the before and after in her battle to take back her life. Deke hung the boarding ladder over the side and helped haul her onboard.

"Mmmm, you're rockin' that footwear tonight," Deke said, lifting his cap and leaning over to give her a quick kiss. "Maybe we should do some dancing in the moonlight." He winked, then returned to the helm to switch on the running lights of the Carolina Skiff.

Katie sat on a cushioned bench in the bow and slipped out of her boots and socks. She wiggled her pink toenails at Deke, then pulled on a pair of leather Top-Siders and tied back her long blonde hair in a ponytail. The boat picked up speed as they headed to Sandy Point, the closest beach for a moonlit picnic.

A Southern boy through and through, Deke had a disarmingly nerdy charm, coupled with a quick wit. He had a kind heart too, the pain of his failed marriage still fresh sometimes, even after seventeen years. But falling in love, if that's what they were doing, churned up a lot of buried feelings, hers closer to the surface. Earlier in the year, Deke had been an expert witness in the environmental lawsuit that ultimately forced Katie's ex-husband to sell the lot next to hers and stop harassing her.

She wasn't sure time really healed all wounds, but she had been keeping Deke at arm's length for too long. After their first kiss in the endless summer of lockdown, things had heated up between them again in May during the cicada emergence, when they had recorded the mating calls of Brood X in Kane's Creek. Katie knew she had to come to terms with the roadblocks she had built around her heart or risk losing him in the process of regaining her ability to trust. But her short-lived third marriage had nearly broken her, and she was afraid to voice her deepest fear.

Am I supposed to feel wholly healed before I try again? If so, I may never be ready.

As if he could hear her thoughts, Deke reached for Katie and guided her to the helm. Standing behind her, he wrapped his arms around her waist and nibbled on her neck as she steered the boat toward the mouth of Belmont Bay.

She was still getting used to his Movember mustache, but he was determined to win the office competition at the science center for best facial hair. November was men's prostate and mental health awareness month, and his male colleagues were growing a beard or mustache—or both—in support of the cause. The mustache was a very good look on him and an even better feeling as he nuzzled the sensitive spot under her ear.

Define "ready." My body certainly is.

When their lips met, it was as if the poison of her last relationship dissipated from her bloodstream, boiling over until it evaporated and left her body entirely. Maybe that was what they meant by sexual healing. Maybe it was time, finally.

Deke had a way of quieting the noise in her head, refocusing her energies on the everyday awe of life. The last time he'd come over for lunch, they had watched in amusement as squirrel after relentless squirrel slid off the birdfeeder into the dogwood tree below. He had assumed his professorial tone and almost convinced her flying squirrels had evolved after the introduction of "squirrel-proof" feeders. When he pulled out his ever-present notecards and lectured her in his slight Southern drawl, she was fairly convinced she had a whole lotta learning left about life—and love—and he was just the man to teach her.

Deke throttled back to bring the boat off plane as they approached shore. In the dimming light, Katie noticed a white head high up on a tree limb in a massive oak.

"Oh, look, one of my bald eagles is here."

Deke chuckled as he bumped the boat in and out of gear, slowly approaching the sandy shoreline.

"Don't you think Mr. Eagle is a bit offended? That's really a misnomer given his full-feathered head."

Katie smiled and shook hers. Deke felt like home, and when he touched her, her insides turned into a languid river on a warm day. All tranquil fluidity. But with two college kids in Katie's house during the pandemic and Deke housing a roommate, it had been hard to find alone time, other than on his open boat. It was definitely getting too cold to get frisky outdoors, however.

Excuses, excuses.

She remembered one of her brother's favorite nautical sayings, "Give wind and tide a chance to change." How Ben could quote polar explorer Admiral Byrd and write complex computer code as the co-founder of a major IT firm was something she often pondered, considering they shared the same DNA. But he was right. She would soon be riding the tide in her new ferryboat. Every day took her further from the past and into her future.

Katie had once been a technology leader like Ben, but after COVID layoffs at the cruise line where she worked in Miami, she had taken a break from corporate life and explored other ways to make a living. With any luck, she could make ends meet on the water. After she completed courses for her captain's license, she planned to run nature tours and shuttle visitors to and from the town of Occoquan and the new inn being built at Bonnie Brae, the "pleasant hill" that had been in her family for more than fifty years.

Katie couldn't wait to tell Deke her latest news—the town's mayor had asked her to lead the holiday boat parade and bring Santa to the town dock to herald the beginning of the holiday season. It felt like the culmination of all her dreams since childhood, when her parents had taken her and her brother there by water and she had fallen in love with Occoquan's riverfront beauty and small-town charm.

Deke beached the boat on the sandy shoreline, part of a protected peninsula within Mason Neck State Park with trails leading deeper into the wetlands. Twilight turned the sky darker shades of blue and purple. Other than a cabin cruiser anchored around the point in Occoquan Bay, they had the beach to themselves.

Deke settled himself on a flat piece of driftwood with his guitar. As Katie grabbed a canvas bag stuffed with blankets, she noticed something gliding in the shallows.

"Hon, look," Katie whispered, pointing toward a beaver.

Before Deke could respond, the beaver slapped its wide, flat tail on the surface of the water.

"Okay, okay," Deke said. "We'll stay away from your den."

The beaver dove under and emerged farther down the beach near a small inlet.

"He must be building his winter home up that creek," Deke said.

"His little ears were so cute," Katie said. "He was watching us long before we noticed him. Did you know Native Americans call this the Beaver Moon?"

"You've been reading your almanac, I see." He smiled and strummed his guitar.

She had also read that the November moon was known as the Mourning Moon, a time to let go of the year's burdens once and for all. Maybe the Beach Bonfire Babes should have a ceremonial ritual to burn off all the negative juju in their lives. Like the periodical cicadas that shed their exoskeletons after thirteen or seventeen years underground, she and her friends could emerge from their pandemic caves in bright new bodies. If only menopausal bodies could do some shedding too. She was still fighting an extra ten pounds on top of last year's ten.

"It won't be long before I have to winterize the boat," Deke said. "We're lucky we got a late bout of Indian Summer this week. The almanac says we're going to have a mild December."

"Well, that's good to hear because, drumroll please . . . the town asked me to lead the holiday boat parade this year. Can you believe it?" Katie uncorked the bottle of wine. "Everything is falling into place for the shop, the inn, and now my ferry service." She poured the rich merlot from nearby Potomac Point Winery into paper cups to toast the moment and handed one to Deke, but he set it in the sand and looked away, not making eye contact with her.

"That's fantastic, babe," he said, but the tone of his voice seemed flat and detached. "They've really embraced your plans."

Katie watched him as he fiddled with his guitar. Instead of celebrating her opportunity to become a part of the town's annual tradition, Deke gazed absently across the water to the far shore.

"Everything okay?" she asked.

"Yeah, yeah," he said, running his hand through his hair distractedly. "We should be able to have your dock and boathouse rebuilt by next summer. Then you'll be in business."

"I even found a space at the town dock for the *Princess of Tides* over the winter," she added. "They've got bubblers, and the river doesn't normally freeze near the dam."

Katie looked across Belmont Bay at the soft glow of lights coming from the river house at Bonnie Brae. Even before she could walk, she had played in the sand on the beach formed between the two jetties of rocks. She imagined grandchildren someday, collecting rocks and fishing for perch and catfish just like she and her brother had.

Katie had finally allowed herself to start dreaming again, and the dreams she had launched on that shore were getting bigger every day. Last week, she and her best friend had started looking at architectural designs for the inn Rhiannon was building on the adjacent land.

And she still longed for a forever love—one like her mom and dad's marriage—but that was one dream she didn't feel worthy of having after all her mistakes. Her friendship with Deke was definitely *something* more, but despite their undeniable attraction, she sometimes wondered if being friends was all she could handle.

CHAPTER 2

MOON RIVER

Deke strummed a few chords, and Katie recognized the opening strains of "Moon River" from one of her parents' favorite movies, *Breakfast at Tiffany's*. She sat next to him as he hummed and tried to remember the lyrics, ad-libbing as he went along.

"I don't think the song actually says 'two *rivers*.'" She chuckled.

"Well, I was thinking of the Potomac and Occoquan Rivers as we sit here at the confluence," he teased, "and how they flow toward the Chesapeake and then to the Atlantic."

"Uh-huh. It's always an educational moment with you," Katie said.

Deke put down the guitar and gestured for her to join him. He pulled her into him and wrapped a flannel blanket around them, cinching it tight so she was nestled in the crook of his arm.

"Actually, Johnny Mercer wrote that song about growing up on a river in Savannah, not far from my old aquarium on

Skidaway Island. He said, as a kid, he felt like a real-life Huck Finn. Will you be my huckleberry captain?" he asked.

Katie giggled. "Mmmm, huckleberry, blueberry, strawberry, Berry Manilow, you name it. I want to be your everything," she joked.

"Cute, but that was Andy Gibb, not Barry Manilow."

"Well, in any event," she said as she snuggled closer to him, "friends first and a little more?"

"Oh, my Katycat, much more."

Deke cupped her face with his big hands and pulled her toward him for a soft kiss that lingered its way into every vein. "You. Are. The. Best. Kisser. It's like we're transferring souls."

"I feel it too," she said, running her fingers through his hair. "And that mustache of yours, wow, it's like one of those weighted blankets on naked skin. It's remarkably soft but with pressure behind it. It feels so damn good."

"Could you just *not* say the word 'naked'? You're the one creating all this pressure." He pulled her even closer, and she felt *exactly* what he wanted her to notice. "Listen, this isn't, well . . . you must know this isn't all about getting in your pants." He kissed her nose, her eyelids, each ear. "I mean, sometimes you wear dresses."

She laughed and practically lunged for his lips again. Their hands explored under the blanket like fervent teenagers trying to make the most of a stolen moment. Finally, he broke the kiss, and she shivered with a mixture of anticipation and the dropping temperature.

He leaned his head into hers so their foreheads were touching.

"Woman, you are making me crazy. I can barely stand how much I want you," he groaned. "When I was, well, quite a bit younger, the backseat of a car was enough. But I'm a little tall for that now. And taking you to a hotel just seems cheap somehow. I was thinking . . ."

Deke paused and smoothed her hair back.

"I think we should plan a trip," he said, somewhat tentatively. "Over the holidays. Just you and me." His eyes searched hers for agreement. "I want to take you to my favorite place on earth and hear the excitement in your voice when—"

Katie interrupted him, trying to sound thankful. And practical. "A trip would be wonderful. I mean, after Belle goes back to school." She hoped he understood she wasn't playing hard to get.

Katie continued, "I'm not going to know what to do with myself when she and Tate are back in New York City for the spring semester. It's only a few more weeks."

Deke pulled back and shook his head, as if to rid himself of the idea and the moment that had been so close to magical. "Yeah, I get it," he said in a low voice.

Do you really?

Katie had managed to keep a lot of men at bay with the demands of parenting as a single mother, and she had lost some over the logistics of being together. But with COVID restrictions lifting, there was an end in sight.

"Listen. I need to tell you something." He leaned back, creating distance between them, and waved the air with a piece of paper from his coat pocket, dissipating what was left of the electricity between them.

Katie stiffened. "Does this come with an index card, professor?" She gestured toward the paper in his hand. In his lectures at the science center and the gallery, he always wrote his talking points in blue and red ink in two columns on a 3x5 card.

"It does actually."

He stopped the frantic fanning and glanced at the writing on the card. She reached for it, but he shook his head and held it out of her reach. He seemed to be debating whether to share the contents of it with her.

"What is it? A pros and cons list of holding out for me?" In five seconds flat, her tone had gone from flirtatious to somber.

There I go ruining the mood again.

Her last marriage had nearly wiped out her self-confidence, along with her boathouse and dock. Sometimes when she looked at herself in the mirror, she questioned whether she had the sex appeal to hold a man's interest . . . or the stamina to survive any more heartbreak.

His voice softened, barely above a whisper, but it was a quiet night without the summer sounds of the cicadas. "Katie, I'm sorry. I'm trying to be funny, and it's coming out all wrong."

He lifted her chin and looked directly into her eyes. In the moonlight, his face had a chiseled ruggedness that bore witness to many days outdoors.

"I'm simply trying to tell you, in no uncertain words, how I feel about you. I want you to know I'm all in for wherever this journey leads us. You're my best kiss. And my last first kiss, I hope." He turned the card around in his hands, displaying three words written in red Sharpie. All caps. "I. Love.

You. I can't *not* love you." He ran a hand through his hair as he looked at her warily, waiting for her response.

She laid her head on his chest, and he wrapped his arms around her, his fingers stroking her hair. "I love you too, Deke."

There. They both had said it.

But instead of fully enjoying the moment, she mulled over his less-than-enthusiastic reaction to the holiday parade. It almost felt like he was trying to ensure her commitment before . . . what? Before he left again? Deke had ghosted her once before, and she was still wary of trusting any man.

Katie pulled back, looking him in the eyes. "Umm, why do I feel like there's something you're not telling me? We're still on track to splash the boat when I take delivery next week, right?"

Her words hung in the air, sounding a little more desperate than she intended.

Deke disengaged and stood up, walking to the water's edge where he picked up a rock and skipped it in the shallows.

"A while ago, I accepted a six-week research opportunity over the holidays. I was hoping you would come for part of the time. Anyway, I'll be back in January before classes are back in session. I'm leaving right after Thanksgiving."

Katie put her elbows on her knees and clasped her hands, biding time before she answered and striving to contain her knee-jerk response.

I don't get this.

She shook her head as she looked down into the sand, as if the tiny granules might explain the man's push-pull approach to their relationship.

"What? You're not spending the holidays with us? I don't understand. I—"

Deke turned around, holding a different index card full of writing. "Look, I've been going to the Galapagos every year since my wife—well, ex-wife—and I split. It was better than trading the kids back and forth and causing a lot of pain. I run the Darwin Institute while the full-time staff members go home for the holidays. They've been depending on me for seventeen years."

He looked down at the card again. Katie stood up, brushing sand off her jeans, and started briskly packing up the food and collecting their trash.

"I guess I made the short list on your card, huh? Do you have notes on how to have a committed relationship or only on how to avoid one?"

Disappointment welled up in her eyes, and she fought for composure while she readied the boat to head back. Her last marriage had been a hard lesson in how lonely she could be in a relationship. She should have known better.

"Katie, this isn't about avoiding anything. I'm a scientist. This is how I live my life."

She picked up the blanket and shook off the sand, folding it as she carefully chose her words. "I'm not expecting you to change your life for me, Deke. But I thought you might want to make a few modifications to fit me into it, that's all."

Before Deke could find a response among his index cards, they were interrupted by a high-pitched scream and a splash much louder than the beaver's tail. They both knew sounds carried a long way on the water, but what they heard seemed extremely close, and the sense of fear in the woman's voice was hard to shake. The water temperature had to be in the fifties that time of year, and Katie didn't want to think about the effects of hypothermia.

"I saw a boat in the cove over there when we pulled up," Katie said urgently, pointing to the south end of the point bordering Occoquan Bay.

Deke ran toward the noise while Katie grabbed the blanket. Just as they rounded the point on foot, carefully making their way over driftwood, a boat passed them on plane, nearly clipping the jetty that extended toward the channel. If not for high tide, the boat might have run aground.

Katie gasped when she saw a woman standing on the shore, shaking her middle finger at the vessel.

"You lousy piece of—"

The boat engine drowned out the rest of the woman's colorful attack.

"Oh my God, are you okay?" Katie approached the woman with the blanket and wrapped it around her. The woman's teeth were chattering, and she was trembling from the cold, but she wasn't crying.

"Oh, honey, we'll get you warmed up in no time. I'm Katie, and that's my . . . umm. That's Deke. I live on the other side of Belmont Bay." She pointed toward the house on the hill.

"Ma'am, are you hurt? Anything bleeding?" Deke asked, coming closer to look her up and down for injuries with the light of his cell phone. "Let's get you back to our boat. You can't be out in this cold air very long."

"No, no, I'm fine. He just hurt my pride, that's all, and probably ruined this new outfit. Damn him! He drinks too much and just loses his mind. I've been trying to get rid of him since lockdown lifted, but he's like a toe fungus. It gets under your nail, and pretty soon you've lost your whole foot."

Katie tried to suppress a laugh, wondering if the woman had a few drinks under her belt too. "Well, that's one way to put it!" she shrieked, her voice carrying across the water.

"I mean, *really*," the woman said. Her short white-blonde hair stuck straight up, but her makeup was still perfect, not a smudge in her bright-red lipstick.

Katie had to give her props for pulling off the wet-dog look impeccably.

"I'm sorry. My name's Kendall. Thanks for coming to my rescue. And that was my boat, *Char-Don-Eh*."

In the distance, the boat barreled up the channel, continuing on plane past the signs for the no-wake zone. Deke stepped away and hit a button on his cell phone, and Katie suspected he was calling the marine patrol. The boats docked in the marinas along Occoquan Channel were in for quite a rocking.

Kendall stared at her mismatched feet and laughed. "Oh, fudge, I lost one of my new boots too." But even bedraggled, she had a smile on her face.

"Sounds like you need to give that dude the boot, no pun intended," Katie said, giving Kendall a squeeze. "The good thing is that you're safe. Let's get you back to my house and warm you up by the fire."

Katie had a feeling that losing a boot was the least of Kendall's worries, but somehow the woman didn't seem worried at all.

CHAPTER 3

RIVER REFUGE

When Katie and Kendall pulled up to the river house, Belle stepped outside to greet the Jeep with Darwin close on her heels. The porch lights illuminated the bordering globes of lavender and goldenrod mums planted by Katie's mother years before. The colonial Cape Cod, with its wide front porch and bookend chimneys, had been Katie's refuge in the storm of her life. She wondered if her past experience could shed any light on Kendall's tumultuous relationship and help her find her way out. As upbeat as she seemed, Kendall might be harboring the same insecurities that had entrapped Katie in her relationship with James.

The Old English sheepdog bounded over to Kendall, and she hooted and bent over to wrap her arms around him. "Is this really a dog? He looks like a stuffed animal come to life. Am I in Disney World?"

As they walked in the door, the welcoming aroma of cinnamon, cloves, and fresh oranges filled the foyer. Katie had called ahead to ask Belle to put out fresh towels and stir

~ 19 ~

the mulled cider Katie had started in the Crock-Pot earlier in the day. The full moon was on display through the two-story, floor-to-ceiling windows in the river room, as if to keep a watchful eye on the women.

"Let me rephrase," Kendall said. "Martha Stewart's version of Disney World. I feel like I've walked into a page of *Southern Living* magazine. Your place is gorgeous, and everything smells so yummy. Even a grandfather clock. I love it."

"Oh, the grandfather clock is just for looks. It doesn't work anymore," Katie said, "but thanks for noticing."

After quick introductions between Kendall, Belle, and Belle's college roommate, Tate, Katie ushered Kendall into the shower. She warmed some cinnamon scones from the local bakery and served them with her mom's favorite clotted cream, or at least the US equivalent of the UK's unpasteurized version.

"You're a lifesaver," Kendall said as she strolled into the great room in a fluffy pink bathrobe, her hair in a towel. "I mean, literally. My cell phone is still on the boat! I would have frozen my ass off overnight without you guys."

"It was dumb luck that we were there," Katie said.

Dumb luck and a lot of desire, she thought, shaking off the memories of her very grown-up make-out session with Deke. Katie pointed toward the closest seat to the fireplace and set a mug on the coffee table. Before Kendall could sit down, Maui stole her place, stretching out on the quilt she had put out for Kendall and beginning to purr.

"Wow, he's a friendly one," Kendall said, picking him up and settling him in her lap.

"He rules the roost around here," Katie said. "Kauai is around here somewhere too. They were my mom's cats, known collectively as the Hawaiians. She named them after her favorite islands."

"Oh, he's a lover boy."

The tiger-striped cat kneaded Kendall's lap as she gingerly took a sip of the steaming cider.

"Mmmm, that's delicious. Got anything to take the edge off?"

This woman is my cup of tea.

"Rum or bourbon?" Katie asked, looking at the options in the liquor cabinet.

Katie normally stuck to wine, if she drank at all these days, but after the night's events, she needed a drink. In a matter of minutes, Deke had told her he loved her, but oh, by the way, he was leaving her . . . again. And then they'd rescued the damsel in distress.

"Yo ho ho, how about some rum?" Kendall cackled in her best pirate-wench voice. "Your daughter's a sweetheart, by the way. I've got a daughter and two grandsons who live near Tampa."

"Grandchildren. How wonderful! You must miss them. The house is going to be too quiet when the girls go back to college in January. They run a dance studio on the third floor." Katie pointed toward the landing. "And they keep this place jumping."

"Oh, to be twentysomething again," Kendall said.

Katie's phone dinged with a message from Deke.

"It's Deke. He says there was an arrest." She looked up, concerned about how Kendall might react, then continued reading. "And police were going to impound the boat but the harbormaster recognized it and let Deke put it back in its slip."

"He deserves that and more, geez," Kendall said. "I hope Larry didn't bang up my boat, or anyone else's, on his way in. Please thank your man for me. I have to figure out a way to extract that asshole from my life."

"Well, I know we don't know each other yet, but you're welcome to stay the night. Or I can take you back to your boat to get your phone. Or home. You live near the marina? Whatever you need. You've been through a lot tonight."

"It's just so nice to relax and feel safe. I'm constantly on pins and needles with that man. I met him on Tinder at the beginning of COVID." Kendall chuckled. "I swiped right, and it was lots of fun at the beginning, but I've been trying to swipe him out the door ever since! It was never meant to last. I just didn't have the heart to kick him out during lockdown."

"I get it. Lockdown had a way of revealing any cracks in a relationship," Katie said. "I found out my husband, now my ex, was cheating on me, among other things. And my best friend found out her husband had a whole other family on the side. He couldn't keep up the facade when he didn't have an excuse to go into the office."

"Oh man, I'm really sorry to hear that. But look at the bright side. You were just 'marry-nating' like a sirloin steak, gettin' all hot and juicy for the right man. And Deke is one tall drink of water. At least you've rebounded well."

Katie nearly fell off the sofa laughing. "Well, that's a story for another day, but I'm gettin' there."

She poured a second round of cocktails, this time with apple brandy.

"If I drink much more of this, one of the girls will have to drive you home," Katie joked.

"Ya know, I think I'm gonna take you up on your offer to spend the night. It's really refreshing to participate in some girl talk. I needed this." Kendall dabbed at her eyes. "I haven't quite figured out my love life since my husband, Don, died. I think I don't know how to be a girlfriend. After a forty-year marriage, I only know how to be a wife, so I just move too damn fast with men. Plus, ever since menopause," she lowered her voice, "I just can't get enough sex! It gets me into trouble, hence this loser. I'm a little older than you, and I'm telling you, you're in for the ride of your life after you ditch those hormones once and for all."

This woman is going to fit right in with the Beach Bonfire Babes.

They skipped the small talk and covered a lifetime's worth of lost loves and boating dreams into the wee hours. Katie was surprised to learn Kendall was a wine enthusiast who had closed her wine shop in Bradenton, Florida, after Don's heart attack. She had moved back to Virginia to be near her daughter, who then turned around and moved to Tampa shortly thereafter.

"And she took my dog with her! Can you believe it? I told her she better bring my Bichon back when she visits in December. Frosty was all I had after Don died. Just when you think you've got your golden years figured out," Kendall said, "there's something else to blow you off course. All I'm saying is, don't wrap your life around that girl up there. She'll find a way to break your heart."

"I was just fortunate to have a little extra time with her," Katie explained. "For the first half of the pandemic, she lived with Tate's family in Maine. Then I got the house cleaned out and put in a dance floor upstairs to lure them here. They're running a small studio and taking classes remotely until next term."

"Just remember she's on her own path now. My daughter's almost thirty, and I'm still telling myself I have to make— or remake—my own life," Kendall lamented. "But you'll get your reward. Just wait until you have grandchildren."

"Well, you didn't expect to be doing it alone."

Katie told her about the grapes she and Rhiannon intended to plant in the spring, if the county approved the rezoning. Rhiannon was getting more frustrated by the day.

"Tell me more about your wine business," Katie said.

"My boat name is *Char-Don-Eh* after my favorite white wine and my husband, who was Canadian, eh? Get it?"

They descended into giggles, repeating "eh" over and over until Belle looked down from the upstairs railing and yelled at them.

"Mom, *seriously*? We're trying to sleep. We have an early class in the morning."

Being reprimanded by her daughter only made them laugh louder. It had been a long time since Katie had let loose and gotten a little tipsy. She had been drinking a bottle a day at the height of quarantine, mourning her mother's death and beating herself up over her bad choice in husbands, at least the third one. It was hard to believe that was only a year ago, but time had taken on a different dimension during COVID, like they had all entered a portal into *Land of the Lost* for a while.

The two women had so much in common, and they quickly went from zero to full throttle, sharing intimate details of their life stories. Not many women piloted their own boats, and they'd both lived in Florida and knew those waters too. It was clear Kendall had a big heart. Katie knew all too well how it felt to be adrift, but she'd found her footing again. And she was determined to help Kendall find hers.

CHAPTER 4

SMALL-TOWN SPIRIT

Mill Street was slumbering when Katie drove into the nearby town of Occoquan early the next morning to meet Chaya and ready the gallery for the artist reception for Danylo. The main street still had the historic air of a commercial district from colonial days, with clapboard and brick storefronts lining a one-way drive that bordered the river of the same name. Every one of the six streets within the tiny town, not even a square mile in size, was festooned with red bows on shop windows and wreaths hung on every lamppost. That evening, the mayor and town council would light the Christmas tree in front of the town hall to kick off the holiday season, and two weeks later, Katie would escort Santa to the town dock on her floating sleigh.

Katie parked in front of the Riverwalk, the Victorian building on Occoquan's boardwalk where her mother had once housed her travel agency, Memories of a Lifetime. It was going to be a special season with much to be thankful for since vaccines made it safe to see loved ones again. Despite

~ 26 ~

the tragic loss of her mother to the virus, she said a silent prayer of thanks that her daughter and friends had made it through the dark times.

Katie felt restless after her conversation with Deke and had barely slept. While her dreams for Bonnie Brae and Bonfire Voices would establish deeper roots in the area, his seemed to take him farther away.

It's only six weeks, Katie. Deal with it.

Deke had moved up from Georgia in the spring when the full-time position at the science center was approved. But how could she have known he was so holiday-averse? She wondered if she could be with a man who didn't seem to appreciate family traditions and desire togetherness at times of thanks and celebration.

Breathe, Katie. It will all sort itself out.

She bundled up and walked to the boardwalk as a single scull glided across the flat surface of the Occoquan River. Through the fog rising from the water, she spotted a great blue heron fishing in the shallows on the opposite bank. The rower approached the nearby boat ramp and kayak launch area, and when he pulled alongside the dock and stood up, she recognized Deke's tall frame and long gait. He lived in an apartment on the top floor of the adjacent Riverwalk.

"Good morning, handsome," Katie said, trying to get back on an even keel with him after her outburst. They hadn't talked or even texted since the night before.

"Hey," Deke grunted, not making eye contact with her.

Sarcasm had a way of robbing a relationship of its lightness, but she thought she had a right to be upset. Katie wasn't sure how hard she wanted to work to get back in his good graces.

"I just dropped Kendall off at her boat. She spent the night . . ." Katie's voice trailed off. "Can I help you put that on the rack?"

"Nope, I got it," he said.

"She lives in the old golf course community across from Belmont Bay," Katie added.

"Who does?"

"Kendall. The woman from last night."

"Oh. Right. Well, I'm glad she's safe and you two had a good night. I gotta get to work." He brushed by her and headed down the boardwalk.

"See you later?" she asked, but he was apparently out of earshot and didn't respond.

As a department chair at the science center, Deke would be introducing Danylo and showcasing plans for his commissioned work. They had talked about going to the tree lighting ceremony after the mural presentation.

Katie regretted her front of sarcasm the night before and the distance it had already put between them after the intimacies they had shared less than twenty-four hours before. At the same time, she wasn't sure she had the energy to pull him out of his man cave again. With a little time, she hoped he would see how his pending departure made her feel.

Chaya was bristling with enough energy for the both of them when Katie walked into the gallery. Her wirehaired dachshund stood on his back legs and pawed at Katie's calves as she admired the transformation of the riverfront space into a holiday wonderland.

"Hey, Bosco."

Katie picked up the sausage-shaped dog and walked around the gallery, admiring Chaya's handiwork while scratching his furry beard. The windows facing the water were draped with festive garlands, and each s'mores station on the high-top tables was encircled with greenery. Chaya was setting up a menorah in the bay window.

"Oh, good, you're tall. I can use your height to hang these snowflakes from the ceiling." Chaya pointed to the folding ladder. "Chop, chop. Time's a wasting."

"I need coffee first, Chaya," Katie said, emphasizing the "k" sound in her childhood friend's name.

Chaya pointed to the Keurig machine. "It's DIY day, girl. What's gotten into you?"

Katie had known Chaya for what seemed like forever. They'd met in Montessori school but didn't really click until first grade when Chaya had consoled Katie after a shocking revelation from another classmate—Santa wasn't real? "My parents say Santa comes to those who believe," Chaya had said. "That girl's a brat, so Santa doesn't come to her house. What does she know?"

Being Jewish, Chaya's parents had never shielded her from the realities of Gentile holiday traditions, but Chaya's heart was big enough to embrace all traditions, and she was always up for a party. Katie knew she was brimming with excitement to welcome Danylo into their community of artists. The fact that he was a single Jewish man upped the ante.

"Deke and I had quite the night—"

"I don't want to hear it," Chaya interrupted flatly. "It's been forever since I've even been on a date."

"Hush. I don't mean it *that* way," Katie said. "We rescued a woman whose boyfriend tossed her overboard and left her for dead. She spent the night at my house."

"Oh, wow. I'm sorry for joking around. Is she okay?"

"Yeah, she seems pretty resilient. Her name's Kendall. I invited her to come tonight. She's a widowed wine distributor who moved up here from the Gulf Coast of Florida. Apparently, this boyfriend of hers came over for a date during COVID—not too safe, if you ask me—and just never left. He's bad news."

"Oh, did he get arrested?" Chaya asked. "I saw something on my local news app this morning. Several boats in the marina got banged up. Larry somebody?"

"That's the one."

The bells on the door jingled, and Rhiannon rushed into the gallery as if her short curly hair, recently colored a burnt red, was on fire. Rhi was one of the newest members of the Beach Bonfire Babes, the growing group of Katie's friends who met on the beach at Bonnie Brae once a month. The six of them found they did their best talking around the circle of flames, when the world disappeared into the black night, and they could focus on their inner lives. The outer circle of life—jobs, children, partners, and often self-imposed responsibilities—had a tendency to take over, but within their circle of friendship, they were reminded of their truest selves.

The soul-searching imposed by quarantine, as well as the impacts of corporate downsizing, had led the group of women to form Bonfire Voices as another income stream. Each had her unique creative or operational talents that contributed to its success. They ran the gathering gallery like a pop-up, bringing in painters like Rhiannon, musicians like Charlotte, artists like Miranda, comedians, authors, and local nature and history experts. Patrons reserved tables with electric s'mores centerpieces where they could roast marshmallows with a charcuterie-like selection of toppings. Ava, the only one of the bunch with any real experience running a business, prepared protein shakes. And Chaya, a former commercial interior decorator, had discovered a knack for event management when workers stopped going into the office.

Rhiannon's coastal paintings adorned the walls of the gallery, awaiting their new home at the B&B she was building next to Bonnie Brae. But zoning complications were trying her patience.

Rhiannon didn't try to keep the door from slamming.

"Good morning to you too," Katie said, eyebrows raised.

"The county development office is driving me batty," Rhiannon said in rapid fire, as if continuing an escalating debate inside her head. "They've reviewed all the plans submitted by my developer for the septic field and footprint of the inn. But they won't put their stamp of approval on it until they do a site inspection, and, of course, they're understaffed because people are still getting sick, even with these vaccinations. So, they moved the site inspection to January, and that could get bumped too!"

Katie was in the midst of making coffee and offered a cup to Rhiannon. "Maybe a shot of Irish cream would help?"

"I wish," Rhiannon said. "I gotta get out of here. I didn't

expect these complications. And I did not expect winter to be so friggin' cold. I stopped by to say goodbye in person. Bonnie and I are headed to Texas to stay with my daughter through New Year's."

Katie was taken aback. Glancing out the front window, she noticed Rhiannon's RV parked along the curb and taking up half the street. Her Jack Russell was peering out the passenger's side window.

"Wow, you're not joking," Katie said. "You're not coming to the tree lighting tonight?"

"And what should we do about your Christmas paint-and-sip session?" Chaya interjected.

Chaya managed all the bookings, and Katie noticed the perturbed expression on her face.

"Oh, crap, I forgot about that. I can do it remote?" Rhiannon offered less than enthusiastically.

Chaya quickly shut down that idea. "I'll just offer a refund or future credit," she snapped. After a few minutes to reflect, she said gently, "Sorry. I know you haven't seen your family in, what, at least a year, other than video chats? The holidays must make you feel the distance even more."

"Ain't that the truth," Rhiannon said, stepping back out into the cold.

"Well, you better make the break now before the Surgeon General changes his mind," Katie said, following her out to the RV to say goodbye to Rhiannon's dog. "Share your location so I can follow you. Darwin's gonna miss you," she teased, rubbing Bonnie behind her ears, "but the Hawaiians not so much."

Katie's Old English sheepdog towered over Bonnie, but they played like they were brother and sister, seemingly unaware of the size discrepancy.

The two women hugged, and Rhiannon's shoulders shook.

"What's so funny?" Katie asked, grasping Rhiannon's arms when she realized her best friend was crying. "Hey, what's going on? Are you sure you're in the right frame of mind to take this trip right now?"

"Yes, this has been building for a while. I just wasn't ready to talk about it. I need some time away to reflect and regroup. I came here right after things ended with Corde a year ago, remember? And I don't feel like things are moving fast enough for me. I need to figure out whether I'm really up to being an innkeeper and, uh, a viticulturalist."

In Rhiannon's Texan twang, the wine-making role came out sounding like sophisticated slang for "over my dead body." Katie fought to show any reaction. The distance she'd sensed from Rhiannon had been real after all, but she had blamed herself. The happier and more in control she felt, the less she leaned on Rhi. They weren't depending on each other like they had when their lives had been in crisis. Katie worried it was one of those friendships that got a person through a season in life but wasn't sustainable over the long haul.

"Oh, Rhi, I had no idea. I'm sorry I wasn't tuned in. Maybe you just need to clear your head, get some inspiration, and start painting again. I bet we'll sell your current inventory while you're gone."

Rhiannon gave a half-hearted smile. "Happy beginnings don't always lead to happy endings. We both know that," she said with a tone of finality, climbing into the RV.

Katie had never seen Rhi so devoid of her usual spunk. She stood in the road, watching her friend drive down Mill Street and out of town. Rhi had been her refuge when Katie's new life had started sinking in Fort Lauderdale, and they'd been quarantine companions for the past year. She was out two best friends for the holidays, it seemed—Rhi and Deke. But with any luck, she would be so busy with the new boat she wouldn't notice their absence.

CHAPTER 5

ALL I WANT FOR CHRISTMAS

Christmas cookie baking was an annual tradition with Belle, but since Katie had moved to the river house, she had lost track of all the old recipes. Belle had found a bunch online, but Christmas cookies didn't taste the same to either of them without Grandma and her mother's secret ingredients. They wanted to make enough treats to freeze for holiday events at the gallery and their personal consumption through the winter. Katie figured there would be a lot of dough and frosting sampling in the process, her favorite part when she had baked with her mom.

After helping Chaya at the gallery all morning, Katie rushed home to spend the afternoon with her daughter. Like most college-age girls, Belle was normally absorbed with school and her roommate, along with their virtual dance school. Bonnie Brae Ballet & Barre had thrived online during the pandemic, and it gave the girls a much-needed outlet for their energy and a safe way to interact socially with the greater community.

Belle was in the kitchen, clearing counter space and getting out baking sheets, when Katie got home. Wearing a crop top and leggings with her hair in a messy bun, she looked like a supermodel who had dropped in from the gym to film a cooking show. Katie gave her a quick hug and kiss on the cheek and refilled her water bottle at the refrigerator.

"I need to take Darwin for a walk first," Katie announced.

"That's fine," Belle said. "I'll change and sort through the cookie cutters for the holiday ones."

"We can wear our matching aprons—the ones you made when they taught you to sew in Girl Scouts," Katie suggested. "Check the tablecloth bin in the upstairs hall closet. I think that's where I stored them."

Belle rolled her eyes. "I'm surprised you still have those old things . . . NOT."

"It's the only way I can preserve a millisecond of time," Katie said. "Before long, you're apt to be a mom yourself."

"No, thank you," Belle said in a singsong voice. "This is *my* time to shine."

Katie watched Darwin's gray rump bounce down the gravel road to the beach at Bonnie Brae. The Hawaiians followed along at a safe distance, their long tales twitching as they avoided wet leaves and mud puddles. With most of the trees bare, Katie could see Belmont Bay along the entire quarter-mile walk. The water was a dark green color, and an osprey chirped high above, circling and flapping its wings as it positioned itself to dive for a fish.

Katie walked along the shore, scouring her brain to remember where she had stored the old recipe cards. Head down, she occasionally squatted to inspect an opalescent quartzite stone, a mottled piece of granite, or a piece of petrified wood. She had not found any arrowheads in a while, not since the trove of artifacts that had kicked off the archaeological investigation last winter. Katie smiled, remembering how one little arrowhead helped her win the battle to save her land—and her heart—from her vengeful ex-husband.

Katie's trip down Pleistocene memory lane was interrupted by the ding of a text message from the Annapolis boat dealer. That must mean my boat's ready, she thought, making a mental note to call back later. She and Deke planned to launch her new twenty-five-foot pontoon boat at the boat ramp at Occoquan Regional Park and take it for a shakedown cruise before winterization—or at least that had been the plan before the news of his sabbatical.

Katie dreamed of establishing a small fleet of open-deck boats, and she had pored over boating magazines and websites, trying to find the right model for the river. When she saw the tritoon for the first time at the boat show in October, she knew it was the right one. The triple-hull pontoons, outfitted with large outboard engines, carried up to sixteen passengers and could safely navigate the shallow creeks and coves of the Potomac. The third, or middle tube, provided greater stability, plus it allowed for a modified V-shaped hull for speed and performance, unlike the traditional two-tube pontoons. Impulsively, she had placed an order on the spot.

Was that only a month ago?

She and Deke had celebrated with painkillers and monstrous roast beef sandwiches—traditional boat show fare—on the rooftop of Pusser's Caribbean Grille overlooking Annapolis City Dock and the spire of the Maryland State House.

The annual in-water boat show was a much-anticipated event held every fall around her birthday, and it was fun to attend with someone who loved powerboating as much as she did. Her brother would often bring his sailboat down from Boston for the sailboat show the following weekend, but Ben had recently moved his boat to a marina in nearby Galesville on the Chesapeake Bay since he was living in India.

"Oh, how I've missed this," Katie said as she slathered her sandwich with horseradish.

"That's fresh horseradish, you know, shaved right off the root, not the cream version," he cautioned.

"Don't I know it," she said, taking a bite.

Deke laughed as the tears ran down her face, and he refilled her water glass multiple times.

Lately, Katie's tears had been from joy and the overwhelming blessings of her new life. A year had passed since the landslide that destroyed the boathouse and everything in it. The settlement she had received from the destruction of land and property was blood money, the only thing she got after her divorce from James other than her freedom and peace of mind. And those were worth a lot more than money. James had been hellbent on taking everything he could from her. But the emotional damage was harder to recover from than she had expected.

As Darwin sniffed along the shoreline, Katie scrolled through her email.

"We regret to inform you that, due to supply chain issues, your order of a 2021 25' Tritoon is delayed. Please contact your dealer to schedule a new delivery date."

She let Darwin off leash while she frantically called her Annapolis dealer. He picked up on the first ring.

"What's going on?" she asked. "This can't be happening."

"That's why I texted you. I hoped you would hear it from me first," Will said. "I've been on the phone all morning trying to find another boat for you on the East Coast. The plant in Indiana can't get all the parts. You wouldn't believe all the backorders."

"But at the boat show you seemed so certain . . ." Katie said, trying not to whine.

"I thought we had found a loophole. I'm really sorry. The good news is they're offering a rebate, and the rest of your payment is delayed until spring," he offered.

"Spring? What?"

Katie barely heard the rest of the conversation, her mind in overdrive. She was kicking herself for being overly optimistic, placing the order before she'd even rebuilt her dock.

What else is new? Two years ago, you rushed into a marriage. Look at where that got you.

She'd rushed into a commitment with a boat, and her aluminum groom had just put on the brakes. Her record for hooking up with the Tin Man had hit a new low.

Katie quickly signed off on the call, resisting the urge to cancel the order altogether. She had been boating on the Potomac on her family's seventeen-foot Boston Whaler her entire life. Her dad would take them up to DC to watch the Fourth of July fireworks from the water with the monuments as a backdrop. Sometimes, they would visit friends further downriver where the water got salty near the Chesapeake

Bay, and she and her brother would sit on the dock, catching crabs with just a line and chicken necks. Ben had been a master at waterskiing antics, kicking off one ski and showing off. They were always competing with other boaters for the biggest boat tube in the bay and had named theirs Big Bertha. She would never have that life—or that boat—again, but she hoped to help her passengers make cherished memories of their own.

Darwin followed a scent along the shoreline, nose close to the colorful pink quartz pebbles and rounded blue-gray rocks that lined the banks of the shallow bay.

Face it, Katie. You're not ready.

She needed to complete the online portion of her master's license and rack up enough on-water experience to take more than six paying passengers. For the past two years, since the dream had germinated, she'd been documenting her sea service time, but she had gotten ahead of herself.

She'd overcome so many setbacks. She just had to put her nose to the ground and sniff out a solution. She didn't want to disappoint the mayor and all the shopkeepers in town who had rooted for her new business. Maybe she could rent a boat for a day.

Give wind and tide a chance.

When Katie and Darwin got back to the house, Belle was sitting on the front porch swing with a thick green book in her lap. She was bundled up in her long puffer coat, her nose red from the cold.

"How was your tick walk?" The incessant arachnids were always Belle's excuse for not walking Darwin. She looked up from the book and surveyed them both. "Mom, what's wrong?"

Katie had a face that always gave away whatever she was feeling. "Oh, just a delay with the boat. And no ticks this time of year. They don't like the cold any more than I do."

She didn't want to ruin the afternoon with Belle by dwelling on it. The pandemic and all its repercussions kept screwing with their lives in one way or another. She should have expected a hiccup.

Belle beamed. "Look what I found!" She held up *The American Woman's Cook Book.*

Katie gasped. "I can't believe you found it!"

"It was with the aprons. You must have stored it there when you were sorting through Grandma's stuff."

They walked inside and started thumbing through it on the kitchen table.

"Look at the date. It's the Wartime Edition."

Belle emphasized the timeframe like it was prehistoric. Meanwhile, Katie had to remind herself the Second World War had happened nearly eighty years ago . . . in the last century. As a family of veterans, wartime history and patriotic events had been a part of her upbringing, a frequent topic of dinner conversations.

Katie laughed. "You make it sound like they were cooking over an open hearth, like Martha Washington at Mount Vernon. They actually had electric ovens, you know."

Katie wondered if the cookbook had been her grandmother's, like the diary she'd found last year from the 1920s.

"Hush, Mother," Belle teased. "You've got to check out this inscription. '*Sept. 4, 1944. To Dorothy and Sourpuss on your wedding day. From Heather.*' Who are these people?"

"I'm guessing Sourpuss was your uncle, the one stationed at Pearl Harbor after the bombing. I know people used to give cookbooks as wedding gifts. Maybe he came home between boot camp and his deployment and quickly got married. Your great grandma had a lot of stories about wartime weddings. Surprisingly, those marriages often made it for the long haul."

Belle flipped to the desserts section, where handwritten recipe cards were inserted into the book. "It's got Grandma's recipes in it! Look at this."

Katie recognized her mother Clara's handwriting and the typed notes made by her grandmother, Elfledia, who had Parkinson's disease later in life and was only able to write using a typewriter. She was surprisingly proficient at the hunt-and-peck method, as she called it, guiding one trembling hand with the other. Where there was a will, there was a way.

Katie gasped again. "Oh, I'm so glad you found this, sweetie. I wondered where all the old recipes went. The cornflake Christmas wreaths. The bells with the little silver candies on them. Oh, and the icebox cookies made in rolls like the packaged dough at the store."

"Can we bake all the family Christmas cookies this year?"

Belle had turned twenty during the pandemic, but in that moment, she had the eager look of an eight-year-old. Katie resisted the urge to wrap her beautiful daughter in her arms. Sometimes her love came across as smothering or overbearing, and she wanted to cherish their time together as long as she could.

"Sure, and we can freeze a bunch so you can take them to school with you . . . so you won't forget home."

Belle would be moving back into her dorm in New York in mid-January to start the second half of her junior year. The pandemic had interrupted freshman year, and her sophomore year had been fully remote.

She bumped her mom with her shoulder. "We can store them in a tin like they used to in the old days—"

"Like before Tupperware and plastic, you mean?" Katie interjected.

"Yes, and I can take them on the train."

Belle read off the ingredients while Katie populated the grocery list on her phone app. "Mom, what's oleo?"

"It's another word for margarine. Apparently, there was a butter shortage during the war, so it makes sense that it's in this edition."

"Bizarre," Belle said as she Googled the substitution. "It looks like we'll just have to watch the time and temperature. Butter has a lower burning point."

"Not a problem," Katie said. "Let's warm up the oven while we wait for the grocery order to arrive. I'll make a batch of popcorn, and we can start making strings of popcorn balls for the eternal tree."

During the months Katie had been alone during lockdown, she had marked time by redecorating her mother's artificial Christmas tree for every holiday. She and Rhiannon had spent hours on the phone searching Amazon and Etsy for strings of colorful eggs for Easter and tricolored ribbon for the Fourth of July, and they had even designed a Mardi Gras tree in yellow and purple for Lent.

Belle gave her an impromptu hug. "Thanks, Mom."

"We can make this an old-fashioned Christmas, cookies and all."

CHAPTER 6

DREIDELS AND DREAMS

Bonfire Voices was standing room only when Katie arrived for the reception. She recognized the town council, other shop owners, and representatives from George Mason University and the Potomac Science Center. As Katie made her way through the crowd to Chaya, her eyes found Deke's, and when she smiled, his expression seemed to soften.

Deke was talking to a man who was very close in height to him, and also extremely handsome, but that was where the similarities ended. While Deke had tousled dirty-blond hair, the other man had finer European features, with a thick head of long black hair tied in a ponytail and a full goatee. Not many men could pull off a mustache, but both of them rocked theirs. Deke strode to the small corner stage to make introductions.

"Sorry I'm late," Katie whispered to Chaya.

Chaya looked gypsy-chic in black leggings, calf-length boots, and a flowy peasant blouse accented by a filigree leaf pendant on a long gold chain from Miranda's upcycled gems collection. Her thick brown hair was pulled into a side braid that framed her face, accentuating her smoky eyes, sharp jawline, and creamy skin. Chaya never seemed to get any wrinkles, not even laugh lines, and she laughed a lot.

"No problem. You just missed your friend, Kendall," Chaya said under her breath.

"She already left?"

"Yeah. She's a hoot. The jail called her to pick up Lockdown Larry," she said with a surprised shrug.

Chaya had a nickname for everyone, and she had certainly come up with that one quickly.

Deke introduced Danylo and shared a short presentation of his international projects. The street artist's giant wildlife art, spray-painted from cranes on the sides of nondescript buildings, took him around the world. His talent with a can was big, bold, and beautiful: a vibrant fox near a power plant in Ukraine, blue jays morphing out of sprayed strokes on a wall in Salt Lake City, multi-colored elephants on the side of a hotel and art space in New York, and even a half-cat, half-tiger on a bomb shelter in Israel. His personal story was just as interesting. He had evaded arrest a number of times before finding a way to make a living with his photorealistic graffiti art. His underlying goal was to raise environmental awareness of how manmade structures could encroach on the natural environment.

Katie looked around the room, noticing the high-top tables decorated with red-and-green checkered tablecloths while the long table filled with families had a blue-and-white runner. Each bay window facing the water had a different theme—Santa's sleigh and his reindeer on a downy bed of artificial snow, a wooden manger with carved figurines, and a menorah surrounded by gold coins and dreidels. Chaya had included relevant books, making each window area into an educational cubby. The mix of religious and secular accents could have clashed, but Chaya somehow made it all work. Outside, children sat cross-legged on the back porch of the gallery, happily entertaining themselves while their parents were inside.

"What are they playing with?" Katie asked Chaya.

"They're paper dreidels," she said. "Right before the reception for Danylo, we hosted a dreidel-making workshop for kids and parents. They loved it. I found some online templates and printed them out. I never knew I was crafty, but I had some help from . . ." She nodded toward Danylo on stage and smiled warmly.

"Wait. Who's 'we'? You and Danylo ran the workshop together?"

"Mm-hmm," Chaya responded slowly, putting her chin on her hands. "He saw me setting up for it and offered to help. He's really, um, nice."

"Nice, uh-huh. And that's code for . . . " Katie winked.

"Anything I can do to get to know that man," she said, motioning toward Danylo.

"Yeah. What's your label for him, or are you still working on that?"

Chaya's expression turned solemn. "It's an ancient Hebrew name. I'm not gonna mess with the name of a biblical prophet."

"You're certainly due for a divine favor."

Chaya had been married once years before, but the big news at the last beach bonfire was that her ex hadn't made it through the pandemic. RIP, Naughty Nico.

Chaya ran her hand over the tablecloth, trying to smooth out the wrinkles. She was clearly holding something back.

"And?" Katie asked, leaning over and nudging her affectionately. "I know there's more."

"He asked me if I'd attend the tree lighting with him," Chaya said, her voice just above a whisper. "And have dinner afterward at D'Rocco's. He made a reservation."

"A man who takes charge—and makes dreidels," Katie commented.

Chaya had been waiting a long time for someone who shared her faith. She had never been the type to chronically date, or even marry, the wrong man. Meanwhile, Katie tended to make things work against all odds, sometimes with disastrous results. Chaya kept to her routine and focused on herself, believing that someday God would look favorably upon her. Katie just hoped Chaya wasn't setting herself up for heartbreak when Danylo returned to Ukraine. But it was the holidays and a nearly full moon, no better time for a little romance.

Katie squeezed Chaya's hand. "I'll come back after the tree lighting and close up the shop. Shoot for the moon." She then added softly, "You're never too old, and it's never too late."

Chaya chuckled, giving her a quick hug. "We're at the point in our lives when we need to take those quotes to heart—and live them!"

Danylo approached and helped Chaya with her coat. As

they walked toward the door together, her childhood bestie turned back to smile and wink.

The gallery emptied out as everyone headed toward the town hall at the other end of the street. Deke had been standing right behind Danylo, and he watched as Katie turned off the tabletop bonfires and shut off the lights. He rocked on his feet and finally spoke to her.

"Still up for some caroling?" he asked.

When their eyes locked, the familiar sense of home washed over her, and he stepped forward.

"Only if I can have a hug first," Katie said. "Look, I'm sorry about my reaction last night. Your plans took me by surprise, and I had hoped . . ." Her voice cracked, and she stopped speaking.

Just yesterday, they had professed their love for each other. But what if he pulled away once she decided she was all in? Was he just another friend for a phase of her life, like Rhiannon seemed to be? She didn't want to believe that, but she had spent way too many hours, maybe even years, over-analyzing relationships. She told herself she wasn't going to fight it if the trip was Deke's way of saying he wasn't ready. The right man would make the effort to communicate.

Deke pulled her into his arms and smoothed her hair, resting his head on top of hers as he held her. "And I'm sorry I didn't tell you earlier about the Galapagos. I kinda wish I could get out of it now."

"It's just as well," Katie said, looking up into Deke's eyes to gauge his reaction. "The boat is delayed until spring. The dealer called me today and—"

"Oh, wow, I wasn't expecting that. I'm so sorry, Katydid. I'd offer the *Sea Bug*, but she's too small for what you need."

And it belongs to the science center, so you would have to be here to pilot it.

"I get it. Anyway, you won't be missing anything."

"That's so *not* true," he said, tracing her bottom lip with his finger. "Darwin's research is pretty fascinating but not nearly as fascinating as you." He lifted her chin. "I know I won't be here for Christmas, but I don't leave until the Sunday after Thanksgiving. If I'm still invited, I wonder if I could help out with the cooking. I've got a smoker in storage. Mind if I bring it over?"

"You'll smoke the turkey?" she asked, nodding her head vigorously in approval. "That would be great. As long as you know how to do it. I can make all the sides. It will be the two of us plus Chaya and Danylo. Belle too, of course, but she won't be eating much since she's having an extra meal at her dad's afterward."

"Are you kidding? We smoke everything that moves in Georgia. People have been smoking meats to preserve them since prehistoric times, but I've definitely got a leg up on the cave men."

"Oh, yes, you do," she said, touching his mustache.

Katie ran her fingers back and forth over it, studying its color and thickness. It was disarmingly charming, and by partially obscuring his upper lip, it drew her eyes to his mouth as he talked. Her mother had always had a thing for Burt Reynold's mustache, and she had almost forgotten her own teenage crush on Tom Selleck and her grown-up crush on Sam Elliott.

But Deke was way more than a crush, and the sensations the mustache alone aroused in her were *very* adult. She wasn't sure the novelty of his mustache would ever wear off.

Deke slowly stepped her backward toward the windows that faced the river and kissed her in the darkened gallery. As the kiss deepened, Katie opened her eyes and noticed he was looking at her in the moonlight. The tune from the night before replayed in her head.

Can we chase the same rainbow?

Katie giggled. "You're supposed to keep your eyes closed when you kiss."

"How did you know mine were open then?" he murmured. "I had to look at you in the moonlight. Your hair has gotten longer since last summer. And your skin is so soft."

He ran a finger over her cheek.

"And I had to look at that sexy mustache of yours. But we're gonna miss the tree lighting," she said softly.

"We might," he said. "But right now I think we're right where we belong."

"You may be right," she whispered as her body molded into his.

Katie had nearly finished cleaning up after the reception and was in the storage room checking supplies for the holiday festival when she heard the gallery door's electronic lock disengage. She rushed into the main room, but before she could announce herself, she saw Chaya standing in the foyer talking in a low voice to Danylo, their hands intertwined. Chaya must have been in a Danylo daze and had forgotten Katie's offer to close up the gallery after the event.

Katie stopped and backed into the shadows when she saw Danylo trail his finger along Chaya's cheek. Chaya closed her eyes and leaned into the palm of his hand, and Katie silently thanked God for a little holiday magic. The couple looked otherworldly in the moonlight, and Katie didn't want to disrupt the ethereal beauty of their moment. Danylo bent to kiss Chaya, and Katie smiled, looking down at her feet and inching her way deeper into the supply closet.

True to nature, however, Katie backed up a little too far. She felt the subtle movement behind her and tried to arrest it with her back, but it was too late. She had managed to dislodge a box of plastic utensils on the shelf behind her. Before she knew it, she was standing in a sea of forks and spoons.

Oh, klutzy Katie.

"Guys, I'm sorry. I was just in here putting some stuff away. I didn't know you were coming back."

The gallery was illuminated in a soft glow by the lights of the Christmas tree, and in the dimly lit room, they couldn't see her face flushed with embarrassment.

Chaya laughed, and Danylo slipped out the front door.

"Oh, it's okay. Danylo was just saying goodnight," she said. "I've got to get home to Bosco, and Danylo has to get an early start on painting tomorrow before we get some rain."

"Well, I apologize," Katie said, smiling sheepishly. "It kinda looked like things were going . . . um . . . well."

"Yeah, we kinda sorta said goodnight all the way down

the street, starting at the tree lighting. Then at the Love sign in River Mill Park. And then on the bridge overlooking the waterfall." Chaya giggled. "Yeah, I'd say 'well' is an understatement."

"I'm happy for you. You're overdue for a little romance."

"I'm overdue for a *lot* of romance," Chaya emphasized. She walked over to the tree and touched a wine cork topped with a red felt Santa hat and a cotton ball for a beard. "Did you see that some of the patrons decorated our tree? These are some of the DIY ornaments from Miranda's workshop last week." She pointed to a dangling string of beads with a crystal at the bottom and an angel made of layered coffee filters.

"Oh my gosh, they're adorable," Katie said. "I love that people like to hang out after our events and make this place their own, you know?"

"Have you seen how they sit out in the rockers on the riverside, reading and drinking coffee for hours?" Chaya stepped away from the tree and looked hard at Katie. "Can I run an idea by you?"

"Well, sure. Want to sit down?"

The two women settled into one of the window benches, looking out on the river that had once been the main thoroughfare to the town. At its heyday in the 1800s, Occoquan had several water-powered flour and cotton mills and the first automated grist mill in the country. And before that, the iron works made iron for use in the Revolutionary War.

"So, any word from Rhiannon?" Chaya asked.

"She texted to say she made it to her daughter's place, but she's been unusually quiet ever since," Katie said. "She went through a lot at the same time I did. Maybe she's having a delayed reaction. We're all ready to get on with life, and I bet as soon as she's vaccinated and gotten her grandbaby fix, she'll find her juju again."

"Well, I'm just gonna say it," Chaya blurted out. "This town has a lot of arts and crafts galleries. What it doesn't have is a bookstore and coffee shop. I—er, we—could still have musicians and readings like we do now, and of course, activities for kids." She paused, studying Katie's face. "If Rhiannon doesn't come back, I want to buy you out and convert this into an independent bookshop. My job as a commercial office designer has completely dried up, and I need something to do full-time when this pandemic is over."

"Wow, Chaya, that's out of left field. But you know I'm a big reader. My parents would bring us here by boat to a little ice cream shop that doesn't exist anymore. It had a book exchange shelf, and I always wished for a real bookstore or library in Occoquan."

"So, you'll think about it?" Chaya asked.

Her eyes fixated on something on the bench behind Katie, and Katie quickly scooted forward. "What?"

"Oh, there's something big and black behind you," Chaya said slowly, still eying the spot where Katie had just been sitting. "But it's not moving. I think you're okay."

Katie jumped up and did a little dance, trying to make sure nothing was on her. She then reached over and picked up an ornament in the shape of a cobweb with a spider on it. "Check this out. I guess one of your crafters made it."

Chaya took it and inspected it. "That's pretty inventive

and a gorgeous piece. Anyway, back to the books." Her comment hung in the air, begging for approval.

"What's to think about? Rhiannon plans to move her paintings to the inn once she gets that going. So, whether she comes back or not, it's a workable idea. But I'm still missing those ice cream cones. I heard the hairdresser is moving full-time to her beach house in the Carolinas. Maybe you could take over the space next door too."

"Even better," Chaya said. "Maybe I could get Ava to run the food part. You know she had to give up her shake shop last year at the height of the pandemic."

"How do we know all these amazing, entrepreneurial women?" Katie asked.

"It's not 'we,' Katie, it's you. You brought us all together and tapped into our hidden talents, like this spider spinning a magical web and catching all of us in it." Chaya held up the spider ornament and stood to go. "Give me a hug, woman." She pulled Katie toward her. "You've completely transformed my life."

The two women held each other. It was a long hug that spanned decades of knowledge about the inner workings of each of their lives, from preschool to first weddings to present day.

"It goes both ways, Chaya," Katie said. "You've transformed mine too. I think we're all starting to come into our own. Coming of age isn't just for young people. I feel like we're starting over again, but with experience."

"Exactly," Chaya said. "With experience *and* money, something none of us had when we used to let ourselves dream so freely." She walked over to the tree and hung the odd spider ornament on a high branch where it sparkled in the moonlight. "Now we can put our dreams into action."

"You know, I feel like we're coming of *middle* age," Katie said, "and it feels damn good."

CHAPTER 7

A RECIPE FOR HOPE

Since Katie had missed Kendall at the previous night's reception, she suggested they meet for Sunday brunch to catch up on life after Larry. Deke had dropped off his smoker, and ever since, she couldn't get barbecue out of her mind. A local place offered an all-you-can-eat buffet of pulled pork, spareribs, muddy spuds, and cornbread. Despite its location in a nondescript mall, there was nothing nondescript about its food. As tempting as unlimited barbecue sounded, it was almost more than her mind, or her waistline, could fathom.

Katie pulled up in Yellowbird and sat in the Jeep for a few minutes, eyes closed, as she gingerly replayed the previous year's fateful visit to Dixie Bones in her head. Right after her mom died at the beginning of the pandemic, Katie had been in line to pick up a chocolate cream pie when she had bumped into her husband—with another woman. He had claimed to be in Vietnam procuring masks and respirators for hospitals, but instead he had been shacked up nearby the entire time.

Rather than suppress the bad memories, Katie found if she allowed herself one last recall, she could put a fresh spin on them while reminding herself how far she had come. In her mind's eye, she already had the pie in her hand. She yanked off his face mask and artfully faceplanted the pie into James's shocked face. She could just see him with whipped cream stuffed up his nose, the pudding-like chocolate oozing into his perfectly blow-dried hair.

Take that, Eagle Slayer.

Oh, but what a waste of a great pie. And Miranda, another sucker for his lies, had become one of her closest friends over the past year. In fact, Katie was wearing one of Miranda's upcycled pink Louis Vuitton beanies with the pom-pom on top. She glanced in the mirror, admiring her own cuteness for a change. She shook the thoughts away and headed inside.

Kendall was seated in a booth, two giant glasses of iced tea at the ready.

"Love the hat, girl! Where did you get that?"

And the conversation and carbs were off and running. After loading up on barbecue, Katie gingerly asked about Larry.

"So, uh, Chaya said you bailed him out? What's up with that, if you don't mind me asking?"

"I just wanted him out of the state. His brother met me at the jail, and I had all his stuff in boxes in my car," Kendall said. "We basically transferred Larry's entire life right in the parking lot, like a drug handoff, and off he went. It's so nice to have my condo all to myself again."

"Lockdown Larry the Loser," Katie remarked. "You can't make this stuff up!"

The women were laughing so hard, they nearly snorted their sweet tea.

"So, what's new with you? Did you see Deke at the reception last night?" Kendall asked.

"Yeah, we're just a little off right now. I was hoping for this dreamy Christmas, our first together, but he's going to be in the Galapagos. It's like a sabbatical he does every Christmas," Katie said, twirling her straw. "I didn't know he wasn't into holidays."

"I'm betting he wasn't into holidays with his ex. You're divorced with a child. You must know what it was like for him. The dads usually get the short end of the stick. Didn't you and Belle's dad have to plan out your grand calendar every year, bartering over Christmas Eve and Christmas morning?" Kendall asked. "That's no fun."

Katie nodded, realizing how far she'd come from her life as a single mom too.

"See, you're already forgetting. But you're a different woman, and both of you are in a different stage in life now. He'll have six weeks to realize he doesn't have to make any tradeoffs anymore. And to feel how much he misses you."

Katie looked sheepish. "I hope you hit the nail on the head."

"It's a grandmother's wisdom, that's all," Kendall said. "At my age, I've seen it all and then some. Don't overthink it."

"Well, on top of that, I just found out my boat's not going to be delivered in time for the boat parade. I've got to dis-invite you on our Christmas cruise and somehow break the news to the town. I'm pretty bummed."

"Well, it's not the end of the world," Kendall said matter-of-factly.

"I know. I just got my hopes up too high. I'd be a happier person if I lowered my expectations," Katie said.

"Not true, not true at all," Kendall said in a dreamy voice, almost like a genie granting her third and final wish. "*Now* I know why we met when we did!"

She was clearly concocting an idea on the fly and leaned across the table, as if they were conspiring to take over the world.

"How many women own and pilot their own boats, huh? You and I are fellow river rats." She paused as if expecting a reaction from Katie. "I've got your back."

"Well, thanks, but I checked into renting a boat, and every-one's either winterized their engines or pulled their boats for the season," Katie lamented.

"Hello? I haven't. I sneak a heater down into the engine room and keep my boat going as long as possible, which is usually until old Harbormaster Jim catches me. And I've got a six-pack captain's license," Kendall said. "If I'm not already your new best friend, I am now."

"Wait! What? Are you kidding me?" Katie jumped up and hugged Kendall across the table, ending up with an elbow of whipped cream from the pie. "You had me at 'captain's license.'"

The woman was like an aqua angel, complete with a boat and a wine connection, every man's dream. And fortunately, after her experience with Lockdown Larry, she seemed to be ready to focus on friendship for a while.

"Listen, I'm doing turkey day with my neighbor, another

widow. We like to think of ourselves as single survivalists. Still alive and kicking! But if you're free the day after Thanksgiving, let's go for a cruise. I'll show you the boat, and we can come up with a plan," she said.

"Perfect. If you're free tonight, you should join us for our last beach bonfire of the year," Katie told her. "All the girls will be there—well, except Rhiannon, the one from my Florida life—and we can talk about boat decorating. They're all so crafty, and the more help we can get, the faster it will come together."

At dusk that evening, the six women piled into Katie's Jeep for the short but steep drive down the gravel road to the water. After hitting every bump and pothole in the road, Kendall was no longer a stranger to the group. In fact, she had practically landed in Chaya's lap.

"Good thing we only brought sandwiches and s'mores stuff," Chaya said. "I thought you fixed the road after the landslide!"

"Well, I did, but we still have an erosion issue until we can install a temporary berm on Rhiannon's lot and start replanting," Katie explained. "The road is almost a lost cause until the county lets us plant the vineyard. The soil doesn't have anything to cling to right now."

The women shook their heads knowingly and spread out along the shoreline to collect twigs and driftwood for the fire. Katie missed the fireflies that lit the night sky with tiny gold pinpricks in summer, but winter had its own serene beauty and a different variety of birds and wildlife. Last week, she and Darwin had come upon a deer with a full rack of antlers on one of their walks. And her Ring camera often picked up foxes and raccoons behind the house. Like Belle, she didn't miss the bugs and humidity.

As the fire took hold and the dry wood crackled, Ava opened their get-together in her usual fashion with a prayer. "Today we offer thanks for our survival, Lord. None of us expected to be faced with a global pandemic and to have our own mortality brought right to our doorsteps. Our world has changed irreversibly as a result, but our bonds of friendship have been our lifelines in our darkest hours."

Katie looked around the blazing fire and made eye contact with each of her friends who had known her mother. Even at eighty, she had seemed too vibrant to be taken by COVID.

Ava continued, "We also thank you for bringing us together again here—on this week of Thanksgiving—and ask that you watch over those of us traveling to see loved ones after such a long time. And we welcome Kendall into our lives. We are blessed by the light and energy she brings to our gathering. In God's name, we pray. Amen."

"Aww. Thanks, guys," Kendall said.

They sat in silence, warming their hands over the crackling fire and watching birds settle in for the night on the still bay. The squawk of Canada geese finally broke the silence, and they loaded up their paper plates with marshmallows, graham crackers, chocolate, and other toppings Charlotte had assembled on the picnic table. In summer, the women often roasted hot dogs first, but the temperatures were dropping, and Katie knew it would be a shorter gathering. She got right to the point.

"Ladies, I invited Kendall because she's a fellow boater. And unlike me, she actually has a boat. Mine is still on order until next spring—"

She was interrupted by a collective groan.

Miranda voiced what everyone was thinking. "Next spring? What about the boat parade?"

"Well," Katie continued, "all is not lost. Kendall has offered to ferry Santa to Occoquan in the boat parade. I wonder if we can get together to decorate the boat a week from today."

Everyone was quick to volunteer, and it didn't take long to decide on wreaths, garlands, and other decorations. Then Miranda reached into a burlap bag by her side and handed each of them a small item wrapped in Bubble Wrap.

"I made something for each of you. You might want to keep them wrapped until you get home since they're a little noisy. I found these in an antique shop. I'll show you mine."

She removed the wrapping from hers to reveal a vintage dinner bell. The handle was in the shape of an owl. She shook it, and the sound carried across the water. A loon answered the call of the bell with a curious, high-pitched hoot.

"They're brass," she said, "and each one is a little different. I tried to select ones that might have special meaning to you, like the Star of David for Chaya. But I'm not going to tell you all of them."

"Oh, that's so sweet, Miranda," said Chaya. "You always find the most unique gifts."

"Well, thank you," Miranda continued. "I was thinking we could ring them at the dock as the boat parade arrives in town."

"Like our own bell choir," Charlotte said.

"And men will want to come ring our bells!" Kendall added.

"Cheers to that," Chaya said.

Katie got up to stoke the fire and smiled at Chaya. They had agreed to discuss the bookstore after Rhiannon returned from the holidays since she had the biggest financial interest in the gallery. But that didn't stop Katie from mentioning the empty space next door. Ava's eyes lit up.

"Gosh, we were so disappointed when we had to close the store at the height of the pandemic," Ava said. "It felt like the end of an era, but we can't *deliver* shakes forever. I like running a small, family-owned business, and I was praying we wouldn't have to give up our dream. Looks like my prayers may be answered."

"Funny how we dream differently when we're older—with boundaries and limits. Ya know?" Kendall mused.

"True," Chaya added. "We dream so big when we're young, like anything's possible."

"Maybe it is before we have bills to pay and mouths to feed," Ava said.

"The wide-eyed optimism of youth," Charlotte said. "By now, we've seen enough of the world to know what's possible and what isn't."

As a lawyer, she had seen more than enough to make anyone lose hope in humanity, but it had only honed her sixth sense for the truth in people.

"I don't think it's just about being realistic," Katie said.

"It's like we've compiled too many 'what ifs' in our heads over the years. We can't see beyond the 'what if it won't work' to embrace the 'what if it will.' We shut down our dreams before we allow them to take root and blossom into a plan."

"Exactly," Chaya interjected. "When we finally have the means to put our dreams into action, we often have too much fear to take the risk."

Kendall sighed. "Are we talking about dreams . . . or about love?"

There was a collective chuckle around the bonfire, and the women bumped shoulders with each other.

"The pandemic was a reality check," Katie said. "Bigger than that, it was a life quake. I had to ask myself, if tomorrow was my last day, am I doing the kind of work that truly feeds my soul? And am I spending my time with people who expand my mind and nurture my heart? I came up short on all those questions, except when it came to you guys. And that's when I started letting myself dream again."

"Speaking of dreaming," Charlotte said, "my band has been invited to perform at an inn in Stowe, Vermont, over the holidays. One of the guys went to college up there and knows the owner. What a breath of fresh air to travel again, and there will be snow."

The Beach Bonfire Babes always ended their get-togethers with a song, and that night's lyrics were especially fitting. Charlotte sang about white Christmases, and they dreamed about the possibilities of an awakened world, just like the one they used to know before the pandemic had changed so much. The treetops glistened in the glow of lights from the river house at the top of the hill. Katie silently thanked her mother for leaving her with the means to dream about a bookstore in Occoquan and a home where her heart had found hope again.

CHAPTER 8

SQUIRREL CASSEROLE

Katie rose early on Thanksgiving morning with a mix of happiness and resignation. Not only was Deke leaving in just a few days, but they had to say goodbye to Tate. After the past year locked down in Virginia with Katie, Belle, and Rhiannon, Belle's roommate and dance school partner was returning to her family in Portland, Maine. While Belle put Tate's bags in the car, Katie hugged the lithe dancer tightly.

"Maybe your parents can put some weight on those bones of yours. You burned every calorie I tried to put in you," Katie teased.

Belle was a more muscular dancer, while Tate had the traditional body of a ballerina. Strong but thin. Tate enjoyed long-distance running, which kept her especially fit. But social distancing inside for the past year, she had discovered an outlet in journaling and started her own blog documenting college life during quarantine. She was planning to talk to her parents about switching her major to creative writing. Katie knew that decision could change the trajectory of Belle and

Tate's futures, and she hoped their friendship would survive the change.

"You've been like a second mom to me," Tate said. "You put the pandemonium in pandemic!"

"Oh, my, I guess I did . . . inadvertently anyway." Katie chuckled, rolling her eyes and shaking her head.

Tate had lived with them through the landslide and environmental trial last year. It was no wonder she thought things were a little chaotic.

"Please give my love to your parents and stay warm up there. Maybe I can visit next summer if you girls work at the Girl Scout camp again."

As the girls drove away, Katie's phone rang with a video call from her brother and his fiancée, Preeti. The pandemic had been especially fortuitous for the couple, who had gotten together when Ben got stuck overseas at the beginning of the global lockdown.

"Hey, guys! Happy Thanksgiving," Katie said, waving at the screen. "How was Diwali?"

They hadn't talked in about a month, but Katie was looking forward to their planned visit from Christmas through New Year's.

"Hey, sis," Ben and Preeti said in unison. The couple was smiling ear to ear, as always, and their happiness was infectious.

It was so unusual to see her brother be that open with anyone, and she was glad he had held out until the right one came along for him. Katie had married every man she had a serious relationship with, but she had sworn off marriage in her future, even if things worked out with Deke.

"Diwali was magical," Ben said, looking at Preeti. "Preeti has a recipe for your collection."

"Yes, this is something you can make for Christmas. It's called besan ladoo. They're little biscuits with edible gold dust on them," she said excitedly. She held up a dish of glistening balls garnished with sliced pistachios that looked like tiny leaves on a golden apple.

"Wow, you can eat gold dust? Where do you buy it? At Tiffany's?" Katie laughed. "Well, I'll just wait until you get here so you can make them. As bad as I am at cooking plain old American dishes, imagine how I would ruin an Indian dish."

Preeti disappeared from the screen, and Ben's face grew serious.

"Oh, no, Ben. You're not coming?" Katie said.

"Katie, we were just there in the spring for Mom's funeral, and there's so much going on right now—the wedding plans, the new office we're establishing in Pune with Preeti's brother . . ." Ben said. "I'm sorry to disappoint you, but it's still kinda risky to travel too, until everyone's vaccinated."

"I know you're right. I just don't want to get to the point where we only see each other for weddings and funerals," Katie said. "I feel like we're reaching that age."

When the call ended, Katie settled in front of the fire with her second cup of coffee, waiting for Belle to return from the airport and Deke to come over to start the smoker. On the mantel was the collection of lighthouses she had finally unpacked, the last of her things from her short-lived Florida life. The tallest one was the Hillsboro Inlet Lighthouse, the one she'd bought when she lived with Rhiannon and Corde in

Pompano Beach. She remembered standing on the sand there and taking a call from her brother when Mom was still alive, before her entire world had come crashing down.

That seemed so long ago, her dream life in "paradise" that had quickly turned from a whirlwind of happiness into pain and humiliation, even for Rhiannon. But Ben had found Preeti, and Katie had met Deke. The difference was Ben and Preeti were spending the holidays together, and Katie and Deke were not.

She heard the front door open and yelled to Belle, "There's coffee, and I got your favorite pumpkin spice creamer."

"Oh, yum. Thanks."

Belle stirred her coffee at the kitchen island, still in checkered flannel pajama bottoms and a hoodie. Both mom and daughter looked up to watch the sun peek over the ridge on the opposite shore. Through the bare treetops, the river took on a peach sheen in the early morning light.

Out of nowhere, Belle jumped back and shrieked, "Mother!"

Katie jumped too, spilling her coffee. "What? What did I do?"

Belle cringed and reached into the sink, gingerly picking up a thick piece of turkey. The marbled flesh bent at one end in a slight L-shape.

"Ew, this dude certainly had a package," Belle said.

"Oh my God, you scared me," Katie replied. "I thought there was something alive in the sink."

Belle giggled and waved the turkey part in the air. "Well, it looks like it had a life of its own."

"You do know that's the turkey's neck, right?" Katie said.

Belle squeezed her eyes shut, and tears rolled down her face as she shook with laughter.

"Ohhhh. That makes a lot more sense now," Belle said, barely able to get the words out. "I was wondering how he hid that thing under all those feathers."

"Oh, geez, clearly I didn't spend enough time with you in the kitchen."

Katie had never enjoyed cooking when she was a single mom juggling a full-time job and long commute. She always joked she only had a kitchen because it came with the house.

Belle joined her on the other leather sofa in the river room and wrapped herself in a blanket as she thumbed through the thick cookbook again. Katie noticed her marking another page with a Post-it note.

"Don't get any more ideas," Katie said. "We have too much food already, and Chaya is bringing her mother's latkes. Her mom is cooking up a batch for us at their retirement home. I invited her parents to come today, but they're elderly and have to limit their exposure until more people are vaccinated. Oh, and the guys are bringing treats from Mom's Apple Pie."

"I call dibs on the cherry pie," Belle exclaimed.

They watched as two squirrels raced around the deck railing. One with an acorn in its mouth leaped into the branches of a tall oak.

"Do you think the squirrels are up there admiring the sunrise like we do?" Katie asked.

Belle laughed. "I think they're discussing food sources and wondering if you're going to keep replacing their corn cobs all winter long."

"You sound like Deke," Katie said. "That one clearly has

been eating too much corn." She pointed to a squirrel clinging to a narrow branch, its belly hanging over the sides.

"Hey," Belle said, "here's a recipe for roast squirrels. You only need three, and that one probably qualifies as two squirrels in one. With this cookbook, we could live off the land."

"Yeah, no thanks," Katie said in a deadpan voice.

"O-M-G. That reminds me of James on the Ring camera," Belle said, "walking along the shore with his rifle like Davy Crockett or Daniel Boone. Remember when he was trying to scare off the nesting eagles with his shotgun?"

"Could we get through one day without a memory of him?" Katie requested. "At least I can be thankful that part of my life is over."

"Hey, at least we can laugh about him now. And aren't you happy you met Deke?" Belle asked, eyeing her mom. "Is he still going to the Galapagos?" Belle had a respect for Deke that had been missing in Katie's short-lived marriage to James Conway Bland III.

"Apparently so. He said he got tired of being odd man out at the holidays after his divorce, so he started avoiding holidays altogether. It was just easier."

"I can see that. You and Dad do okay, setting aside your differences at the holidays. Maybe if you show Deke how we do holidays, he'll change his plans," Belle said.

"Well, he leaves Sunday, so there's not going to be much chance to show him," Katie said.

But maybe Belle had a point. She could work toward changing Deke's perspective. After three marriages—and three divorces—Katie's heart was like a lost-and-found box for discarded hopes and dreams. She could help Deke find the ones he had set aside, dig them out of the box he'd locked them in, and shake out the wrinkles. Tradition was tradition because it stood the test of time. They could put their own spin on the holidays, replacing the old painful memories with new ones.

CHAPTER 9

FOREVER THANKFUL

Hours later, the house was transformed by the delicious smells of thyme, rosemary, and sage emanating from the deck. Deke wore a red apron bearing the words, "I smoke meat, and I know things." The Hawaiians roamed around his legs, waiting for an occasional scrap.

Katie giggled as she watched him carefully monitoring the time and temperature of the smoker. Every time he came over to the house, he found something to tinker with, and he had insisted on putting a metal thermometer in her oven to calibrate the temperature with the digital clock. As it turned out, the reading was off by thirty degrees, which was an easy way to explain away the casseroles she routinely burned.

As she readied everything in the kitchen, Katie would look up occasionally and spy him watching her. Each time she caught him, he quickly averted his eyes and busied himself with the smoker again. With the cornbread in a cast-iron skillet in the oven and the herb stuffing in the Crock-Pot, she stepped outside to bring him a carving board for the turkey. She held it as he carefully transferred the bird from the smoker.

"You look very manly in that apron, Dr. Kinnebrook," she teased.

"Well, you look very wifely, I mean, uh, womanly in yours, I must say," he said. "I was admiring how you look in a kitchen. Or anywhere for that matter."

Her breath caught. His eyes were filled with warmth and love, so much like the looks that would pass between her dad and mom. She turned away, and he touched her arm.

"You okay?" he said. "I only meant that as a compliment."

"I know, I know," Katie said. "I just miss my mom and dad. They had a love for the ages, you know? Holidays bring it all back. I set the table the same way she always did on special occasions."

"My mom would have loved you," Deke said. "You pay attention to the little things, just like she did. One year she spent almost nine months painting a Nativity scene. This wasn't a paint-by-numbers set. She bought the ceramic figurines, picked out the paints at the craft store, and later took them all to a kiln to be cured. It was quite a project. I just found the crèche when I was unpacking. I'll have to show it to you . . . well, when I get back, I guess."

Katie gave a half smile, wishing she could put his impending departure out of her mind. It was so rare for Deke to give her a peek into his life, and when he did, she wanted to throw open the door and tear it off the hinges so she could see it all. She longed to understand the loving, gentle man and to get under the strong, calm surface he portrayed to the world.

They were interrupted by the sound of the doorbell.

"Oh, that must be Chaya and Danylo," Katie said. "She offered to pick him up."

"Of course she did," Deke said. He leaned in for a quick kiss. "The turkey just needs to sit for a few more minutes, and then I can start carving."

"Pass the applesauce please," Danylo said, after topping his latkes with a big heap of sour cream. He nodded at Chaya. "This is a special treat. My mother would be impressed."

Katie noticed Danylo's hand brushing Chaya's as she handed him the bowl of applesauce.

"I like the Thanksgiving meal to be a hodgepodge of our favorite recipes, not necessarily the traditional ones," Katie said.

"Do you celebrate Thanksgiving in Ukraine?" Belle asked.

Danylo chuckled. "No, no, it's an American holiday, the Pilgrims and all that. But we do have St. Nicholas Day. It comes before Orthodox Christmas and starts the holiday festivities. St. Nicholas leaves treats for children the night before, and everyone visits relatives."

"Sounds like a good way to keep Santa separate from Christmas and Jesus's birth, not mixing it all up on the same day," Katie said, forgetting that Chaya and Danylo didn't celebrate Christmas. "Oops, you celebrate Hanukkah, so they're already separate."

Chaya nearly snorted her sparkling cider. "I didn't do a very good job of teaching you Jewish tradition, did I?"

Deke interjected. "Everyone's got the Thanksgiving story

confused too. It's not really about food, as wonderful as all of this is." He gestured toward the spread that filled the middle of the long table: pumpkin soup, Deke's smoked turkey, Chaya's crispy potato latkes, sweet potatoes topped with coconut and chopped nuts, stuffing, green beans, cranberry dressing, and Katie's Southern-style cornbread.

"The first Thanksgiving wasn't actually at Plymouth," Deke said. "It was at Berkeley Plantation right here in Virginia. English settlers arrived on the shores of the James River, south of us near Richmond, a year before the Pilgrims landed at Plymouth Rock. Thanksgiving was about prayer then. They gave thanks for surviving the journey across the Atlantic, not celebrating the harvest."

Katie smiled at Deke across the table. "We should acknowledge how much we've all survived in the past two years. None of us were untouched by the pandemic." Katie's voice broke, remembering her mom, and she noticed Belle wiping a tear from her eye.

She looked around the table, set with her mother's china, silver, and crystal. Katie's mother, Clara, had treasured her American Limoges china, a white porcelain Eucalyptus pattern edged in silver plate. She had added to her place settings over the years until she had a set of twelve. Katie used the nice dishes and beloved sterling silver—the fittingly named Eternally Yours pattern—on special occasions or when she just wanted to add a little dazzle to daily life.

Katie raised her handblown crystal Tiffin Dolores water goblet. Two years ago, she wouldn't have known, or even cared, about her mom's delicate dinnerware. But understanding what mattered to her mom made Katie feel closer to her and to her parents' lifelong love. While Katie had moved through her life in chapters, discarding what wasn't working for her—from furniture to marriages—as she had turned another page, her parents had imbued all the little things with meaning. When Katie was left to clean out the river house during lockdown, she had discovered many of the objects meticulously recorded in *A Bride's Notebook* in her mother's perfect cursive script.

Her parents had held onto what seemed like everything through the years, like the ties that built and bound them together in their forever love. Maybe by never cutting those ties, never letting go of where they had started, their love became an indestructible foundation of memories, supporting them from their beginning to their end. Surrounded by the remnants of her parents' relationship and immersed in the natural world on the shores of the Potomac, Katie felt the broken pieces of her heart realigning, starting to form a whole again.

At the other end of the dining room table, Deke raised his glass and mouthed the words "I love you" in clear view of her friends and her daughter. At the same time, Danylo took Chaya's hand and casually held it on the table between their place settings. Both Danylo and Chaya stared intently at their intertwined fingers, as if the entire world had fallen away in that moment.

Katie remembered when Deke had placed an arrowhead in the palm of her hand, the first time they'd ever touched. She hoped Danylo and Chaya could open their hearts to love more easily than she and Deke had so far.

CHAPTER 10

A GRAVY BOAT FOR TWO

As the sun set that evening, Deke and Katie watched the blue flames in the center of the fire table on the back deck, which spanned the width of the house overlooking the water. Twilight settled over Belmont Bay, and Jupiter and Saturn appeared as two bright spots in the sky. The eerie cry of a fox disturbed the otherwise silent night, and Brigid and Darwin lifted their heads from their slumber on high alert.

"I hope my story about Thanksgiving didn't put off anyone," Deke said. "Everyone bolted pretty fast after dessert."

Katie laughed. "Well, Belle needed to get to her dad's, and Chaya and Danylo seem to only have eyes for each other right now."

"You know, President Lincoln originally established a national day of thanksgiving during the Civil War to try to unite the two sides," Deke explained. "It's hard to re-envision the parable we've all been taught."

"I didn't know that," Katie said, closing her eyes and focusing on Deke's fingers stroking her hand. "You know a little bit about everything, babe, like a walking Wikipedia."

Deke chuckled. "I don't know everything, but I know I love you, and that's everything to me."

She snuggled closer into the crook of his arm, and he kissed her hair.

"Today meant a lot to me," Deke said. "I know you think I have an aversion to holidays, but I just couldn't bear the awkwardness. If the kids were with me, they missed Mom's green bean casserole or some other tradition I never thought of as a man, you know? If I was invited to their mom's house, which used to be *my* house, I felt like I didn't belong, especially after she remarried. I gave up holidays so my kids wouldn't feel uncomfortable."

"That makes sense, I guess, but I hate to think of you being alone at all the times when people are celebrating family," Katie said. "You don't have to be alone anymore, Deke. I hope you know that."

Deke squeezed her hand, and she turned to face him, pressing her forehead against his.

"Although your turkey carving skills are a little rusty," she whispered gently.

"Yeah, I kinda massacred it. Didn't I?" His deep voice was low, full of the same yearning she felt every time they were together. "Will you let me make it up to you?"

Her body trembled at the desire in his voice. They were just feet from her bedroom, and she stood up and turned off the gas fire.

"Warm enough?" he asked.

"I could be warmer," she said. She let the dogs into the kitchen, then turned back to Deke. "Have you ever seen the moon from this vantage point over here?" She walked backward toward the far side of the deck where French doors led into the master bedroom.

I'm probably too old for a come-hither look.

She leaned against the railing and faced the darkness of the woods. Now that she felt ready to take their relationship a step further, she wondered whether he would turn away.

"I have not," Deke said as he approached her, "but I was going to ask you if I could bring over my telescope."

He stood behind her and pressed his chest against her back. Then he lifted the hair off one side of her neck and said, "You have much better views over here." His lips pressed gentle kisses under her ear. "What time does Belle get home?"

He pulled aside the neck of her sweater and tickled her shoulder with his mustache. Then his hands ran down the length of her arms and moved to her waist, and she felt his thumbs exploring the sides of her stomach under her sweater.

Katie tried to respond, but her voice had somehow fallen into the well of desire Deke stirred inside her. "Tomorrow," she managed to eke out as she turned and wrapped her arms around his neck, her lips on his, her tongue welcoming his into her mouth. She longed to take all of him into her body, her life, her soul.

"Tomorrow? As in after tonight?" he clarified.

"Yes, in the morning. She's spending the night at her dad's house. Do you want to come inside?"

She was nearly breathless when she led him through the door into her bedroom. She had unlocked the door earlier . . . just in case. Inside the room, she switched on the gas fireplace, which bathed the room in a soft, warm glow.

"Your skin. Your hair. They're so beautiful," he said, stroking her face and pulling her toward him for an ever-deeper kiss. With tiny steps, they slowly orchestrated themselves toward the bed where they lay down next to each other.

"Deke, I, uh, I'm probably not like the women you're used to being with . . ."

She felt so self-conscious about her weight these days, especially the accumulation around her middle, and her doctor had told her that her estrogen levels put her in the late stage of menopause. She couldn't seem to rid herself of the belly fat, no matter what she did.

"The women I'm used to being with," he said, "like Brigid? You don't have as much fur, if that's what you mean."

Katie giggled.

"Can you not feel *this*?" Deke said, as he caressed her face with soft kisses. She could definitely feel his interest as he pressed his tall, lean frame firmly against her.

Without any forethought, she moved her hips even closer to him, her body controlled by some primeval instinct.

He grinned and met her movement. "Mmmm. Well, yes, *that*," he said. He rolled her over onto her back and lay on top of her, still fully clothed. "But I mean, when we touch. It's not just chemistry between us. It's everything . . . chemistry, biology, physics. Like the merger of all the integrative natural sciences. So how can I begin to compare you to anyone else when . . ."

Katie closed her eyes, basking in his words and the way he made her feel so wanted. He paused to pull her sweater over her head and begin a trail of kisses from her navel to her breasts.

"We create this fusion that is uniquely ours," he finished.

Straddling her waist, he sat up and removed his shirt. She ran her hands over his shoulders and the muscular curves of his chest.

"This thing you call fusion," she whispered, "I call belonging." She unhooked the front closure on her bra and slipped it off her arms, watching his face as he took in the curves of her body in the firelight.

As he leaned over to kiss her, so much skin touching skin, he said softly, "I promise you, Katie Kat. Our physical bodies are only the smallest part of this whole equation."

CHAPTER 11

CRAB SHACK SHAKEDOWN

"Hey, girl, I was beginning to wonder whether you were still coming." Kendall peeked out of a panel of the clear plastic canopy covering the cockpit of the *Char-Don-Eh* and yelled to Katie as she unloaded a cooler from her Jeep.

Katie tried to deflect Kendall's scrutinizing look, wondering if she had managed to hide the just-crawled-out-of-bed-with-the-man-of-my-dreams look. "Wait until you see the leftovers I packed for our floating lunch," Katie said as she dragged the cooler down the ramp of the floating dock. "Anyway, what's the hurry? We're the only people crazy enough to be on the water today."

The sky was a dull light blue with thin, wispy cirrus clouds high above, and the temperatures were in the forties. At least there wasn't any wind.

"You got that right," Kendall said, laughing and pulling her in for a hug.

Kendall wore a white down coat that was almost the same

color as her platinum hair, cinched at the waist with a belt and gold-plated buckle. Her sunglass frames were studded with pink rhinestones and matched her pink boat shoes trimmed with even brighter pink flowers. She looked like a floating glamour shot. Or maybe a very cute snow cone.

Katie felt underdressed in her lined yellow windbreaker and matching overalls. Compared to Kendall, she looked like a duck hunter, or the Gorton's Fisherman, and she wore an auto-inflating personal flotation device over her jacket. Better to be safe than sorry if she fell in.

"Love your floral Sperry's. But no socks?" Katie asked. "Aren't your toes going to freeze?"

"I'm a Floridian through and through. I can't wear socks. My feet revolt when I do."

The engine was already rumbling, and Kendall helped Katie load her boat bag and cooler onto the thirty-two-foot Chris-Craft, stowing her duffel in the cabin below.

"Let's get this show on the road," Kendall said, engaging the dual throttles and pulling out of the slip.

Katie settled into the first mate's chair and watched Kendall expertly maneuver the engine controls, turning the boat on a dime as they made their way out of the marina. Kendall blew an extended horn blast to announce they were entering the channel, but there was no one around to notice except the ever-grumpy harbormaster, who seemed nonplussed, and a few ducks who took off in the opposite direction toward the town of Occoquan.

As soon as Katie saw open water ahead, she felt a centering calm overtake her. As much as she had questioned the logic of pursuing a livelihood on the water, her gut told her to keep chasing that feeling. Her former IT career had paid the bills, but managing the reservation system for a major cruise line had been an energy drain for her, the price of 'suck-cess.' During the pandemic lockdown, she'd had a lot of time to think about what really mattered to her and where—and with whom—she truly belonged. In her dying days, her mother had cautioned her to be deliberate about how she used her time, to put her energy toward people and pursuits that would feed her soul.

When they reached the end of the Occoquan River's no-wake zone, Kendall zipped the vinyl window closed and asked, "You ready?"

Katie nodded, and Kendall pushed the throttle forward. The boat responded immediately, its bow gracefully lifting off the water in seconds as they glided between Craney Island and the Occoquan Bay National Wildlife Refuge, past Sandy Point where the women had first met, and toward the Potomac River. As they passed Belmont Bay, Katie spotted the red roof and chimneys of her river house on the ridge.

She moved to the aft bench and looked out of a flap in the boat's canvas and vinyl canopy at the wake they were leaving. The only sounds were the water slapping the hull and the two powerful engines. An errant seagull tried to keep up with them. Katie felt the boat turn slightly to starboard as Kendall set her sights on the powerlines near Possum Point.

"Where are we going?" Katie asked, taking a seat next to Kendall at the helm.

"It's a surprise," she said with a sly smile and a wink. "The Beach Bonfire Babes inspired me the other night with all that talk about dreaming big again, and I want to run an idea by you." She glanced at Katie. "You look happy, by the way."

Katie realized she hadn't stopped smiling since they'd hit cruising speed at 3,500 RPMs. "Oh, it seems we've both got dreams up our sleeves. I can't wait to hear this."

The river widened as they cruised through Occoquan Bay and passed into the Potomac River, bordered by the state of Maryland on one side. Katie scanned the shoreline as they neared the Virginia side of the river and pulled into a large cove formed by the powerline station and Leesylvania State Park. She noticed a couple of abandoned white buildings with red shutters and a dock that had fallen into disrepair.

"Hey, isn't that the old crab shack? Tim's Rivershore?" Katie asked. "I haven't been here since Belle was little. I heard it didn't make it through the pandemic."

Miss Rivershore, the ferry that used to take people back and forth between the town of Occoquan and the restaurant, had been gone even longer. She missed the river of her youth, before development and competition had driven out the small businesses that made their livelihood on these waters.

"That's right. The owner still has another location down-river and one on Lake Anna, but he couldn't keep this one afloat," Kendall said.

"Such a shame." Katie shook her head as she eyed the old tiki bar. "We used to come here for the Not-on-the-Fourth-of-July Fireworks."

"It was an icon on this part of the river," Kendall said. "One of the few places where a boater could really feel at home, ya know?"

Kendall idled the boat and started to pull toward the dock.

"Are you sure this is safe . . . and we're allowed to be here?" Katie was skeptical about trespassing. Around there, someone could have a shotgun at the ready or at least an angry dog. And who knew how sturdy the dock was.

"Aren't you the worrywart? We'll just tie up here and have lunch. No harm done."

Kendall pulled the boat alongside the wooden dock, wrapping a line around a piling and then cleating it at the bow and doing the same at the stern of the boat. The triangle of lines held the boat in place while a fender at midship kept the fiberglass from banging against the wooden post.

Katie opened the cooler and unloaded turkey salad sandwiches and a thermos of pumpkin soup onto the round table in the center of the cockpit. "Soups are just about the only thing I like to cook, my favorite meal in the fall and winter. We had too much food last night, so I saved this batch of pumpkin soup just for you. It's seasoned with ginger, nutmeg, and a little bit of creamed sherry," she said, pouring a cup for Kendall. "Oh, I almost forgot. We ran out of cranberry sauce, so I substituted cranberry juice instead. Hope that's okay."

Kendall tilted her head and stared at the bottle of juice. "Am I supposed to pour it over top of the sandwich . . . or dip it?"

Katie pulled a bottle of prosecco out of the cooler. "No, silly, you're supposed to mix it with this."

"Ahhh! I knew we would be besties the minute I met you," Kendall said. "But you can take off that life jacket thingy now, Captain Safety."

Katie laughed and removed her PFD. She then reached into the bottom of the cooler and retrieved a domed plastic container. "And no day drinking is complete without a Wegman's white cake."

Kendall nearly fell off the helm bench. "Wow, this is quite a celebration." She pried off the plastic lid and stuck her finger in the frosting.

"Here's to new friends." Katie toasted with the cranberry mimosa. "May we always be at the helm—of our boats and our lives."

"Indeed!" Kendall said, drinking her champagne flute in one gulp. "One and done! No more for me since I'm driving. Can I show you my secret now? We just have to go for a little walk."

The women stepped onto the bow and then carefully climbed over the rail onto the long dock. As they made their way toward shore, keeping an eye out for loose boards, they walked over names carved into the dock in 2003 when volunteers helped the owner rebuild after Hurricane Isabel. Kendall wiped her eyes when they got to the end of the dock and stared at what was left of the restaurant and Timbuktu, a beachfront bar.

"Don and I had a lot of fun at this place back in the day," Kendall said. "It makes me miss him even more."

Katie squeezed Kendall's hand. "Some losses never get easier, even when you think you've moved on, but at least you have good memories of him."

"Yeah, I shouldn't have tarnished them with Larry the Loser," Kendall said. "I should have sucked it up and been lonely instead of filling space with him."

"I get it," Katie said. "I filled space with James after Belle went to college. But there's a big difference between having company and having true companionship."

Making love to Deke the night before had been like a meeting of their minds, not just their bodies. Together they had become one life force for a while, as if every fiber of their beings intertwined.

How can it feel so right with Deke? So much like forever?

All morning, she had replayed every moment, every soft touch and whispered word. Waking up in his arms made her imagine a future—

Kendall interrupted Katie's thoughts, the ones she needed to forget about anyway. She had made enough mistakes with men, and she wasn't going down that same road of broken dreams again.

"I've been wanting to honor Don somehow, and I think I've figured out how I want to do it," Kendall said.

Katie didn't realize the day was going to turn into a solemn remembrance ceremony. "Oh, gosh. Did you bring his ashes?"

"Uh, no, those are on my mantel," Kendall said matter-of-factly. "But I've had my eye on this place for a while, ever since I sold our wine business and moved back up here. I've decided to buy it."

Katie stepped back and removed her sunglasses. "You're what? Take off those shades. I need to see if you're just joking with me."

Kendall turned to face her and put her glasses on the top of her head. "I'm dead serious. No pun intended. I did a lot of thinking the other night after the bonfire. I mean, what's stopping me?" Kendall put her hands on her hips as she shifted into business mode. "But only if you'll make this a stop on your ferry service. I need a way to bring customers here, and there isn't a ton of parking along the railroad tracks. I brought you here to ask you if we could, maybe, combine our dreams and form a partnership."

All the women in Katie's life seemed to have hit "take charge" mode at the same time. Losing friends and family members during the pandemic had been a reality check that time might run out. While youth had been about dreams with little experience, this later-in-life stage was about dreaming with dollars—and credit scores—and owning their destinies. The Beach Bonfire Babes had bonded together to launch the gallery in Occoquan, and she and Rhiannon had teamed up on the B&B and vineyard. Then serendipity had brought Kendall into her life.

"Holy shit, Kendall. Are you serious?" Katie grabbed her friend's elbows. The ferry service wasn't hard to imagine. She could run a triangular circuit between town, the inn and future tasting room, and the crab shack. "Can you really do this?"

"I don't see why not," Kendall said.

The women jumped up and down, hooting and hollering with abandon, until Kendall's shoe caught on a loose board. Katie watched helplessly as Kendall began to topple off the dock.

"Oh no. Oh no. Oh no," Kendall shrieked as she fell back toward the sand near the water's edge. Somehow, she managed a soft roll when she landed. Tears of laughter ran down her face.

When Katie realized Kendall was okay, she couldn't hold back either. "You're a crazy woman," she howled. "I better get back to the boat before I pee my pants."

A deep voice behind them interrupted their revelry. "Not as crazy as you might think," the man said.

Is he looking at the same woman I am?

In the sand, Kendall looked like a giant roll of cotton candy topped with brown sugar. "Oh my God. Oh my God. Oh my God," she said, trying to catch her breath and stop laughing while also gawking unabashedly at the broad-shouldered man reaching out a hand to help her up.

When she got to her feet, Kendall brushed off her coat and composed herself enough to make an introduction. "Katie, this is Cole Campbell. He's going to be my general contractor. I met him at Madigan's."

"At Madigan's? When?" Katie would have remembered that story.

Kendall shrugged. "Yesterday, Nancy Drew. I'd had enough of mourning with my neighbor last night and went to Madigan's for a drink. Cole and I met at the bar, and we kinda hatched this plan. What can I say?"

Cole looked like the kind of general contractor who wasn't afraid to get his hands dirty with his sculpted, tattooed arms and deep tan. His spiked blond hair made him look like Kendall's giant twin, the Gym Rat Ken to her Boater Barbie. And he was clearly taken with Kendall, his eyes absorbing every inch of her from head to toe.

"No explanation needed," Katie said with a wink.

Wow, she moves fast, but I don't blame her.

Katie considered the logic of mixing business with pleasure, but at their age, throwing caution to the wind felt more like chasing the last rays of sunset. Strike while the iron was hot, as they said, and it was clear from the way they looked at each other that the iron was getting hotter between them with every passing minute.

Grinning and flashing pearly white teeth, Cole said, "This little lady is a powerhouse, as you can clearly see." He winked at Kendall. "I've been hoping someone would grab this place. I've already drafted a bunch of plans, but I couldn't put all the pieces together or all the funds. I think together this could be a match made in heaven . . . or at least as close to heaven as the Potomac River is."

"Well, that's pretty close, if you ask me," Katie replied. "Are you going to keep the same name? I mean, I know you've only had a few hours to think it through."

The way Kendall and Cole looked at each other, Katie wasn't sure whether they had spent all those hours actually planning a restaurant. Maybe Katie hadn't been the only one having a little gravy with her turkey.

"No, a different name. In fact, I've already got a vision," Kendall said.

Of course she does. This woman is unstoppable.

"I want it to be more upscale tiki, you know? We're closer to DC than the crab shacks downriver. I'm not saying I don't love a rum cocktail from time to time, but pitchers of beer aren't really my thing, although I'll sell them. But if you've got a vineyard started across the way," Kendall pointed toward Belmont Bay, "we should name it with the future in mind. I still want it to be a downhome place where you can get crabs and hushpuppies, but it will also have surf-and-turf entrees, like the old Pilot House Restaurant that used to be on Neabsco Creek. Remember that place? I waitressed there in my twenties."

Kendall was talking a million miles a minute, her eyes flashing with excitement, and she reached out and grabbed Katie's wrist and Cole's bicep.

"So, what do you all think of 'Bonfire Blue,' for blue crabs, but without the 'e' on the end. 'Bonfire' to stick with the bonfire theme you've got going in Occoquan. And, just between us, 'BLU' in all caps stands for 'Best Life Unyet.' We haven't lived it yet, get it? We'll paint over all this red in shades of blue," she said.

"Hey, any waterfront restaurant is my kind of place," Cole said, "particularly if you're running the show."

"Bonfire BLU works for me," Katie said. "I mean, there are a lot of details—permits, chefs, staff—but you've run a business before, so you know the complexities. And you can't depend on the boater crowd in the winter. But if you're thinking a seasonal place, it's workable."

"I intend to spend the offseason in Florida with my grandsons," Kendall said, "so that works fine with my semi-retirement plan."

"Plus, the access by car and parking for this place leave a lot to be desired," Cole added.

As if to prove Cole's point, a car bounded across the railroad tracks at high speed, the sound of metal scaping metal as the undercarriage struck the tracks. Kendall stepped closer to Cole as the car approached them, an old, baby-blue El Camino that fishtailed into the small parking lot. The driver made no effort to slow down and seemed intent on stirring up as much dust and gravel as possible to cause a disturbance. When the car finally came to a stop, one side of the front bumper was dislodged and rested on the ground.

With Cole's muscular frame between her and the car, Katie had to rely on the vile string of expletives coming from the car's open window to ascertain who the driver was.

"Oh, shit," Kendall said. "Larry's back! What the . . . ?"

Cole started toward the car.

"Cole, wait!" Kendall tried to stop him, but he was already out of reach.

"How does he know you're here?" Katie asked.

"I must have done a little too much drunken texting on Thanksgiving. It wasn't my best day. He knew I was looking at this place, but I don't know how he knew I was here. Unless he's keeping tabs on me somehow."

"He seems a bit, uh, moody. Is he always like this? Have you thought about getting a restraining order?" Katie asked.

The women watched from a safe distance as Cole approached the car, hands on his hips. There was a harsh exchange of words, and Cole gestured for Larry to turn the car around and head back up the road to the highway.

"I'm only here to see Kendall," Larry yelled. "Just let me talk to Kendall, and I'll leave."

"Oh, give me a break," Kendall said under her breath. She took a step forward, but Katie grabbed her arm forcefully.

"Kendall doesn't want to see you," Cole said loudly. "Now get on out of here before I call the police and you end up back in jail."

Kendall turned and gazed at the flat, calm river. She had been so excited just moments before, but she suddenly looked defeated.

"I'll call his brother and make sure he keeps him on a tighter leash. I'm really embarrassed," Kendall said, then quickly headed for the boat while Katie and Cole watched Larry drive away.

Katie thanked Cole for defusing the situation.

"Hey, no problem. Looks like Kendall's upset, but that dude is clearly unstable. She needs to stop trying to reason with him. Please tell her I'll call her later," he said, kicking at some gravel. "I haven't known her long, but she's got a heart of gold. Maybe you can help her see she deserves better."

"I'm working on it," Katie said, frowning. "I'll give her your message."

CHAPTER 12

DECK THE HULL

With only a week until the boat parade, Kendall and Katie needed to put their plan into action. Fortunately, all the Beach Bonfire Babes were back in town after Thanksgiving. Even Belle had cleared her schedule to hang out with the women and help decorate the *Char-Don-Eh*.

As Katie drove over the Route 1 bridge from Bonnie Brae toward Belmont Bay Marina in nearby Woodbridge, she looked downriver at the tranquil waters of the Occoquan. It was hard to believe part of the bridge had collapsed after Hurricane Agnes in 1972. Before the bridge, the Mason family had managed a ferry across that stretch of river to connect the Potomac Path, once an Indian path that became the King's Highway during colonial days. George Washington nearly drowned in 1791 when his horses and carriage fell off the ferry into the water. The ferry was replaced by a wooden bridge that gave Woodbridge its name.

The docks lacked their usual bustle in late November. Recreational boating on the Potomac was popular from April through October, and many boat owners had pulled theirs out of the water for the winter and stored them in warehouses or on blocks or trailers in parking lots. Under a gray sky with low stratus clouds, the marina wore a cloak of melancholy as the remaining boats settled in for their five-month slumber, blanketed in white covers of shrink-wrapped plastic to keep out rain and snow.

Katie slipped on her work gloves and filled a dock cart with decorations, trying to find the motivation to work outside. It didn't help that she would be saying goodbye to Deke that evening. She perked up at the sounds of holiday music carrying across the water, and as she got closer to *Char-Don-Eh*, she noticed a big set of waterproof speakers secured to the radar arch.

The boat was crawling with people. Belle was hanging a red ball over the bow light like Rudolph's nose. Charlotte lay on her back, stringing lights along the bow rail, her long red hair splayed on the deck. And Deke and Cole maneuvered an inflatable set of reindeer along the portside deck, the side that would face the town when they carried Santa upriver.

Miranda, dressed in a red sweater and jean coveralls patched with festive squares, welcomed her onboard with a quick hug. "Whaddya think?" she said, gesturing toward her hand-sewn red and green boat cushion covers. She was the craftiest of the bunch.

Katie had to raise her voice to be heard over the melody to "Rockin' Around the Christmas Tree." She replied, "You guys have outdone yourselves."

Ava appeared from the galley below with a tray full of seasonal meal replacement shakes. "We've got Christmas

Crack," she said proudly, pointing to a healthy protein shake garnished with sea salt sprinkles and a drizzle of caramel. "Or Frozen Hot Chocolate. Or if you'd rather have something hot, I made a batch of Bah Humbug Tea in a thermos."

"Hey, Mom, it's about time you showed up," Belle said, jumping into the cockpit and grabbing the Christmas Crack out of Katie's hand. "The early bird!"

Katie laughed and took the non-dairy chocolate milkshake, which was her favorite anyway. Since she had started substituting a two-hundred calorie shake for a meal each day, she had noticed the scale moving in her favor. "You're a lifesaver," she said, hugging Ava and giving her an extra squeeze.

Ava had attended the same church as Katie's mom and had been the one to break the news of Clara's passing to Katie, even before the doctors knew to label it a COVID-related death.

Katie glanced around looking for Kendall and noticed her on shore, just leaving the marina office. The flashing Christmas ornaments hanging from each earlobe didn't match Kendall's mood. She had her head down and appeared to be muttering to herself.

"What's going on?" Katie asked, giving Deke a quick peck as he helped her up onto the bow. "Mmmm, you taste like hot chocolate."

His mustache still had a spot of whipped cream on it, and she went in for another kiss. Deke grinned and wiped his mouth.

"She put up some ornaments last night, and when she got back to the boat this morning, they were smashed on the dock. She went to ask the harbormaster to check the cameras and the gate access."

"Oh, wow, that's pretty mean-spirited for the holidays. I wonder if it's Loser Larry again." Or James, Katie thought. No one had heard from Katie's ex since he'd moved out of Miranda's house and sold the land next door to Katie. She often wondered if he would come back to haunt her, but she knew Miranda would tell her if she heard anything.

"You look like you could use a hot toddy," Katie said as Kendall stepped aboard the boat.

"Yeah, that and an electric fireplace. It's gotten colder today. Did Cole unpack it yet?"

Cole, who was surprisingly good-natured at taking orders from Kendall, yelled from the bow. "No, Captain, it's still in the box. I just finished mounting reindeer."

Katie stifled a laugh at the snapshot in her mind and gave a side-eyed look to Kendall, who was doing all she could not to burst out laughing herself.

"Alrighty then! I'm glad to see you got your sense of humor back," Katie said. "But you got a fireplace for the boat?"

"Yeah, an electric one, but I'm not going to plug it in. It seems like it would be a fire hazard," Kendall said. "We're just going to position it on the bow along with a fake tree, some presents, and a big chair for Santa to sit in as we approach town."

"It's really coming together. I brought some greens and red bows to drape around the radar arch," Katie said. "Did Chaya decide not to come?"

"Uh, notice anyone *else* missing?" Deke said, a grin on his face.

Recognition dawned on Katie as she realized Danylo hadn't shown up either.

"She picked him up this morning, but somehow they got lost on the way from town," he said.

Occoquan was only about three miles away by car and an even shorter distance by water.

Kendall motioned for Katie to take a walk with her to the end of the dock. "Listen, I've got a problem." She pulled a metal disk out of her pocket. "Larry put an air tag on my boat. That's how he knew where we were yesterday. I scoured the boat stem to stern this morning and found it in the lazarette, the locker where I store all my fenders."

"I can't believe it. Did you tell the harbormaster? And Cole?"

"I don't want to burden Cole with this right now. He offered to install some cameras, and I might take him up on that. But I don't want Cole to think I'm a flake, and this thing with Larry makes me look like a fool. I think my man-picker is broken."

"I know that feeling all too well, but you're not a fool," Katie said. "You just trusted the wrong guy. Been there, done that."

Kendall paced the narrow dock from one end to the other.

"Hey, can you stop moving for a minute? I'm worried you're going to end up in the water again," Katie warned. "Sit on the dock box here, and try to calm down."

"The marina can't do anything without evidence," Kendall lamented. "The dock gate wasn't accessed last night, so whoever messed with my boat ornaments did it from the water. But somehow, he evaded the cameras. They're only on the ends of the docks."

"You mean he snuck in here by boat, like a kayak or something?" A chill ran through Katie as they sat side by side looking out toward Belmont Bay.

"This is really putting a damper on the holidays," Kendall said. "The thing I hate the most is not being in control, and Larry knows it. What if he comes back some night this week and destroys all our hard work? I think I'm gonna sleep on the boat until the parade. I can run the heater with shore power."

"That worries me even more, Kendall. You've already winterized the head, so you've got to walk all the way to the marina office to use the facilities, and the docks get slick when it's close to freezing. And confronting him could be dangerous, assuming it's him."

Katie wondered again if James had come back to mess with her, but she kept her thoughts to herself. Occoquan had been promoting Santa's arrival by boat on social media, a nice plug for Katie and the gallery, but it meant everyone knew their plans.

"Listen, I can come camp out with you," Katie said. "You've got two berths, and Belle can take care of the dogs. Deke's boxer is staying with us for the next six weeks, but we only have to make it through six more nights."

Kendall nodded in agreement. Her eyes met Katie's, and she finally allowed herself to smile.

"I'd like that actually. We can watch Hallmark movies while we plan the future for Bonfire BLU. I put in my offer yesterday."

"Way to go!" Katie said. "Maybe floating slumber parties

can become our own holiday tradition. I'll pick up some more cake."

Kendall whooped.

"And I'll bring the chardonnay!"

CHAPTER 13

SAME OLD LANG SYNE

Katie didn't want to spend any more time in the great outdoors. She didn't want to sleep on a thin mattress in cramped quarters on Kendall's boat without a bathroom. And most of all, she didn't want to say goodbye to Deke. The afternoon decorating the boat had chilled her to the bone, and she had spent too much time thinking about the similarities between her ex and Larry and worrying about what that could mean for Kendall. Larry might be harmless, or like James, he might have deeper motives.

Deke sounded harried when they talked too. After helping with the boat, he'd gone directly to the science center to tie up loose ends. By the time he'd extracted himself from work, he had little time left to pack. Katie kept replaying the night spent in his arms, but she didn't want their unmatched physical connection to confuse the pending reality of his departure and what it could mean for their future.

"Babe, why don't I just swing by when you're ready," Katie said, trying to sound upbeat when they talked on his drive back to his apartment. "We missed the town tree lighting last weekend. We can walk up to River Mill Park and check out the tree on the way."

A part of her wanted to avoid the evening altogether, and another part wanted to cling to Deke and beg him not to go. If only she could push a button and fast forward to January, but that would mean Belle would be gone. Dropping her daughter off at college had been hard enough the first time, before all the other unanticipated hard things that came after that. She could only hope that COVID vaccinations worked, and she wasn't putting Belle at greater risk being in New York City again.

Katie promised Kendall she'd head over to the marina after dropping off the dog with Belle. Back home, she packed a small overnight bag and put it in the Jeep. Brigid nearly wiggled out of her leash when she saw Katie drive up to the Riverwalk.

"Oh boy! Oh boy! Oh boy!" Katie said, trying to match the dog's excitement as Brigid boxed her legs, her docked tail spinning like a top. Katie squatted down and rubbed the dog's floppy brown ears, so much cuter than the traditional cropped style. "Wait until she sees Darwin at the house," Katie said to Deke. "They're going to wear each other out running up and down the hill to the water."

"I really appreciate you keeping her at your place," Deke said. "I swear, I'm jealous of my own dog. She gets to hang out at Camp Katie with Darwin, and the playground for grown-ups is even better."

His tone was reminiscent of the playfulness of their night together, but Katie didn't feel playful. She took Brigid's leash in her hand.

"I hate to board her," he continued, "and Danylo is working really long days, trying to make the best of good weather."

They walked behind the Victorian building of shops and apartments to the town dock, which ran along the riverfront to Mamie Davis Park. Twilight cast long purple shadows over the river. Passing the gazebo, they wound their way through the small park and headed up the waterfront street of 18th-century storefronts. They crossed the street at the town hall to admire the decorated spruce tree that was nearly as tall as the building.

"I'm glad we came tonight when it's not a mob scene," Katie said. "Check out the ornaments. They were created by a local artist and are 'sold'"—she used air quotes—"in the town's shops to support a local homeless shelter. They must have received a lot of donations this year."

Katie walked around the tree, studying the various designs. "I keep seeing spiders everywhere this year. Look." She pointed to a web-like ornament with a black spider in the middle.

"Hmmm. Maybe it's left over from Halloween?" Deke suggested.

"Strange. I don't think they decorate it like my eternal tree."

Brigid led them up the street to where it ended in River Mill Park at the far west end of town and not far from the dam that formed the Occoquan Reservoir, the drinking water for much of Northern Virginia and a recreational area for non-motorized boating and fishing. A small footbridge spanned the Occoquan River, leading to a waterfall on the other side, and they stopped part of the way across it, watching the water flow downriver past town and toward the Potomac.

Back on land, Deke studied Katie's face in the glow from the flickering streetlight, which resembled an old-fashioned gas lantern. They had barely spoken or touched on their walk, and it was nearly over. He shrugged his shoulders and shook his head, clearly frustrated with her. "I don't know what more to say, Katie. I can tell you're upset, but this is work, not a vacation. It's not like I planned this trip to avoid being with you."

Are you sure?

Katie felt robbed of romance in what should have been their first holiday season together, but there was no point in rehashing the inevitable. "I'm tired, that's all. And cold. Let's keep moving."

Brigid seemed to sense the collective mood and lost interest in walking. As night fell, they sat on a bench overlooking the river, which was rockier and more turbulent just below the dam.

"Science involves research, Katie, and research sometimes means going into the field. I can't always excavate artifacts on the lot next door to yours and come over for lunch every day. All I'm asking for is a little support."

"Don't lecture me," she snapped. "I'm taking care of your dog."

His head jerked back. "I see. So, this is how you want to leave things for six weeks?"

Katie chuckled, her sarcasm rising to the surface again. "*I'm* not the one leaving."

"Got it," he said, standing up and walking over to the railing. His back was to her, hands in his pants pockets, and she wanted nothing more than to stand up and find solace in his tall, sturdy frame. But something stopped her.

"I'm sorry, Deke. I'm just having trouble wrapping my head around this. I had no idea you planned to avoid Christmas for the rest of your life," she continued reluctantly, her next words low and measured. "I'm not sure I can live with that."

There. She'd said it. The words she had feared the most. She didn't want their relationship to end, but she couldn't imagine holidays without seeing *The Nutcracker*, visiting the National Tree near The White House, and sitting in George Washington's pew on Christmas Eve at Pohick Church. She wanted to share her Washingtonian traditions with the man she loved, the same captivating man who would rather be off the coast of Ecuador on another continent.

Deke turned around and removed an index card from his pants pocket. When Katie saw it, she put her head in her hands, reconciling herself to the inevitable. She emboldened herself not to fight it. She would let him walk away.

"Katie, I told you I planned this trip long before I knew where our relationship was going. And frankly, right now, I'm not sure where it's headed. I've told you over and over how I feel about you."

Actions speak louder than words.

She had learned that lesson the hard way. How many times had she fallen for the lines James had fed her on a silver platter. But Katie knew she shouldn't make comparisons. Deke wasn't a big talker. He always seemed earnest and sincere, and she had never caught him in a lie.

Deke continued as if he could read her mind. "I don't know what else to do or say, Katie." He paused, then he approached her. "The other night was . . . well, indescribable."

Katie nodded her head. He was right. More than right. Making love had been like an out-of-body experience. Their connection went so far beyond the physical into another realm where she felt free to touch and explore and feel every sensation without any reservations.

"I hate to say this, but I don't feel like you're meeting me halfway," Deke continued. "I keep telling myself that it's not about me or even about us. I want to believe that you can work through whatever's holding you back."

He ran a hand through his hair and looked at her, his eyes imploring her to understand. To let go of her fears and love him back. He glanced back at his index card. "I'm no neuro-scientist, but I think you're afraid to trust your own feelings. I know you've had a hard go of it, and God knows it took me a good, long cicada life to work my way out of *my* emotional cave. But, Katie, I need to know if you're gonna get there with me."

He bent down in front of her and stroked her hair as she continued staring at the ground. "Are you?"

Deke's words hung in the air. He always had a way of gently and deftly reaching into her soul, of knowing her even before she knew herself. Their impasse wasn't really about Christmas, although it sounded like a page out of the Grinch. She had to risk heartache to reap the rewards. Even though she had told him she loved him, she'd been keeping him at arm's length emotionally. And while she had let him in physically, the tender passion of that connection only amplified the missing piece—trust.

She looked up, and Deke's eyes implored her to reciprocate the intensity of his feelings. But she couldn't do it. She wasn't upset with him. She was upset with herself and the fears holding her back. "Deke, every time I try to love someone, I get it wrong. I'm not sure I know how to get it right or if I ever will . . ."

Her voice trailed off. Deke looked crestfallen and stood and faced the water, while Katie took Brigid's leash and walked past him back to Yellowbird, the dog close at her heels.

Deke caught up with them at the Jeep. He opened the back door for Brigid, and Katie waited while he gave the dog a big hug and kiss.

"Be good for Mommy—I mean, Katie," he said, patting Brigid's head before shutting the door.

Katie stood on the curb, looking at Deke for the last time in 2021. She tried to make her words count, but she didn't know how to explain how she felt. "Deke, I've screwed up so many times. How do I know—"

"Katie, we're not going to solve this tonight," he interrupted, shaking his head and looking at his watch. Then he bent over and put his hands on the hood of the Jeep, as if in surrender. "I just hope you'll give this some thought while I'm away. I will come back to you with no defenses, my guard down. I've lived in a fortress of my own making ever since my last marriage seventeen years ago. I'll give you my heart . . . and every holiday . . . if you can give me the same."

Katie approached him, and he straightened and handed her the index card from his pocket. She folded herself into him, taking in his clean scent, his firm chest, and the sense of belonging that always washed over her when she was in his arms. His lips found hers, and they kissed like it was the first time again—or possibly the last—softly, hesitantly, and with the same question of forever on their lips. She was going to miss that mustache.

Can we face our mistakes and still be deserving of a beautiful life? And a beautiful love?

"You're a sight for sore eyes," Kendall said, opening the dock gate for Katie and taking in her mismatched outfit of Ugg boots, baggy sweats, and a hoodie.

"I'm sorry it's so late. I came as soon as I dropped off Brigid," Katie said. "Belle's going to kill me when she finds out I'm wearing her favorite boots. I was freezing and just threw on the warmest, comfy clothes I could find."

"No biggie. I'm a night owl anyway. Well, how did it go with your scientist?"

Katie burst into tears the minute they stepped aboard the *Char-Don-Eh*. "I think it's over," she blubbered, trying to get the words out.

"I figured it wouldn't be easy, but I don't believe that," Kendall said, wrapping her in a hug and patting her back. She ushered Katie into the cozy cabin, where a mug of lavender tea waited for her.

Katie settled into the berth in the aft cabin, an open area at the back of the boat. When her sniffling turned into wailing, Kendall threw a box of tissues toward her. The box bounced off the stairs that separated the secondary sleeping quarters from the rest of the interior cabin, and Katie crawled across the carpeted floor to grab it. "I know I'm acting like a sixteen-year-old. I'm so sorry."

Kendall chuckled and tucked herself under the covers of the elevated master berth in the V-shaped bow. "Isn't it nice that we can still feel like we're sixteen, even if sometimes those feelings aren't the good ones? We can dissect this later after you get some perspective. It's after midnight. Tonight, you need sleep."

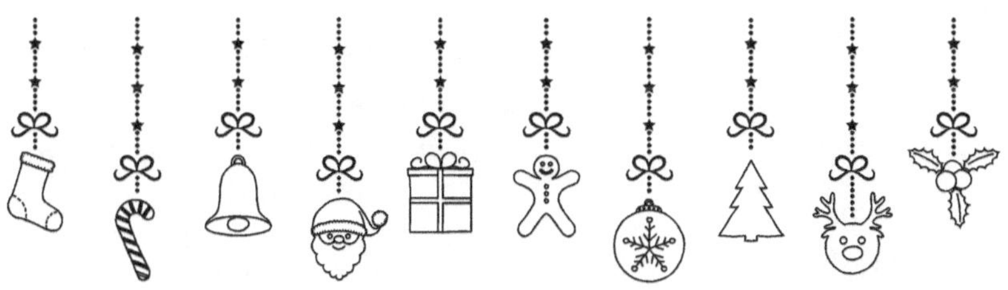

CHAPTER 14

CAPTAIN'S ORDERS

The week leading up to the boat parade was quiet and uneventful, no sign of any stalking exes, and the women settled into a comfortable routine living on the boat. In the mornings, they brewed fresh coffee and sat on the bow in flannel sleeping bags, watching the world awaken. At sunrise, a great blue heron walked the dock, its long spindly legs making carefully orchestrated steps as it studied the water's surface for ripples. During the day, they took turns staying on the boat while one went home to catch up on work and chores. And in the evenings, they made popcorn in the microwave and watched Christmas movies. At night, the only sounds were the gurgling water as the boat swayed in the slip and the haunting call of a loon.

With little else to distract them, they got to know each other *and* the variety of ducks in the marina—common mallards, buffleheads with their little white caps, stiff-tailed ruddy ducks, and hooded mergansers with their oversized heads.

"The tundra swans should be here soon," Katie said. "I hope they're still in the area when Deke gets back."

"That's the first time you've said his name all week," Kendall remarked.

"He hasn't texted all week," Katie said, looking at her phone again for the twentieth time that morning. She and Deke had always texted at the beginning and end of every day and often talked in between his meetings or classes. He'd become embedded in her daily life.

I'm gonna lose him.

Katie wrapped her arms around her knees and held back the tears just behind her eyes.

"God knows, I'm the worst person to be in limbo," Kendall said. "My whole relationship history has been like a Ferris wheel. I'm either riding up the exciting side or losing my stomach down the other. Don and I managed to stay at the top for a good long ride, but I haven't found a way to stop the rotation. I have to give you credit for giving each other some space."

"You think 2,800 miles is *space*?"

"I do," Kendall replied emphatically. "You and Deke have been taking it pretty slow. You didn't just jump right back into a full-blown relationship after your last marriage. It's very grown-up of you. But it seems to me there are still some loose ends *you* need to tie up, the remnants of your pain."

Katie whined. "I don't feel very grown-up. Half the time all I want to do is jump into bed with him." She didn't mention they finally had. "But with Belle in the house, I was trying to behave. Who's to say where we'd be if I had free reign like the last time." As soon as Katie had gotten a taste of freedom as an empty nester, she'd married the first man who came long. Her whole life had gone from sunshine to shit in a matter of months.

Suddenly, a loud boom disturbed the serenity, and Katie's mug almost ended up in the water.

"Damn duck hunters," Kendall said.

They both stood up and noticed a duck blind close to shore.

"I just don't get it. I know it's all about managing the population, but have you ever cooked a duck? You end up breaking a few teeth trying to sift gunshot out of your mouth."

"Oh, I can't stand it," Katie said, shaking her head. "Don't tell me!"

"Cole told me he's got his own duck blind near his place in Colonial Beach." Kendall lowered her voice. "I always wondered what a duck blind looks like inside."

"Uh-huh. His duck blind and what else?" Katie teased.

On Thursday evening, two days before the boat parade, a few diehard boaters met for a captain's meeting at the marina office to discuss logistics for the short cruise into town. The group consisted of local officials, the owner of a local boat club, one duck hunter in a camouflage jumpsuit with his wife, a young family who owned a small electric boat, and an older couple with a trawler named *High Cotton* who were headed to Florida for the winter right after the parade. Kendall stood at the front of the room wearing an irresistibly ugly holiday sweater and dangling red and green earrings shaped like buoys.

Despite the small turnout, Katie and Kendall were happy to have local support, including the county's red fireboat that would bring up the rear like a floating caboose. Katie recognized some of the officials from the Department of Wildlife Resources who had supported her land battle against her ex the previous year.

"Hi, Officer Kessler, good to see you again," Katie said.

"Hello, ma'am. Heard from Deke?"

Deke worked with all the environmental officials on the river.

"He texted when he got to Ecuador. That's all. I assume he's on a little island playing with penguins." Katie tried to tone down the annoyance in her voice, but the smirk on the officer's face made it clear she'd failed.

"I'm sorry to hear your boat order got delayed," he said. Word always got around fast in the boating community. Officer Kessler had been the first to find the *Potomac Princess* washed up on Craney Island after the landslide, and he knew how much she wanted to be back at the helm of her own boat. "Seems like you're in good hands here with Kendall. We go way back."

"Oh yeah?"

Kendall stepped forward, giving the DWR officer a hug. "Randy used to date my daughter when they were in high school," Kendall said. "He's like family."

"How's Alexis?" he asked.

"She's married with two little ones now and living in Tampa. They're flying in tonight and plan to meet us at the town dock. The boys are so excited to see Santa."

After determining fueling and the order of boats, Kendall raised the most important item on the agenda. "And now for the final order of business, who is going to be our Santa?" Kendall asked. "The costume is on my boat, along with some overalls that come with a pillow sewn into them."

The flotilla director from the Coast Guard Auxiliary spoke up. "Herb will do it, and he's got the right belly for it."

"No pillow necessary," someone offered.

The director waited for the corroborative laughter to die down before continuing. "Herb will be here Saturday morning bright and early. He's always punctual."

That night, Kendall and Katie reviewed the plans again, ensuring Santa would arrive in town on the stroke of ten o'clock. When Kendall shut off the overhead light, the cabin was bathed in a milky glow coming from the porthole windows that lined both sides of the cabin.

"Do you think we should take watches tonight?" Katie asked. "If Larry's going to do anything, this is his last chance."

"I think we're overthinking this," Kendall said. "Plus, it's too cold to sit up in the cockpit. Cole attached motion-activated cameras to the pilings of my slip. We'll hear the Ring alert if anyone is out there."

"Okay," Katie said warily. She lay in the darkness, staring at the low ceiling just inches from her face. All she could think about was Deke and his patient approach to life, from the way he described paleontology to his slow, languid kisses and the way he made love, as if every moment counted. "Kendall, you still awake?"

"Uh, yeah, I am. You want to tell ghost stories? Or talk about your first kiss?"

Katie laughed. The past few days had felt like one big high school sleepover, with the modern addition of microwavable popcorn and streaming movies. Although Kendall was in her mid-sixties, she followed the latest fashions and seemed more like a social influencer than a grandmother. Her buoyant personality took over every room, and while she never held back her opinions, she shared them in a nonjudgmental way.

"I'm guessing you want to talk about Deke," Kendall suggested.

"How did you know?" Katie asked.

"Maybe because you've been moping around here like a lost dog all week."

"So, you *really* don't think it's over?" Katie asked. She propped her head up on one hand, elbow bent and resting on the mattress, straining to see Kendall in the dim light.

"I really, really don't. From what you've told me, Deke has been clear about where he stands and what he wants. You were both changed by relationships, but that's life. Our experiences affect us. It seems like Deke became a guarded person for a long time after his heart was broken, but hasn't he come a long way? Not only geographically—moving here from Georgia—but emotionally. And whether you want to accept it or not, you changed because of your relationship with James."

Katie sat up, bumping her head on the ceiling. "Ouch, that was stupid." She crawled out of the berth and sat on the steps leading up to the cockpit.

"Kendall, I don't want to give James that power over me . . . the power to change me."

"Then take back your power over that change, woman. Flip the switch," Kendall said. "James isn't here anymore, but right now he's living rent-free in your head. Decide what's worth keeping—the lessons learned—and discard what's not helping you anymore and what's holding you back from love."

"You make it sound so easy."

"No, I know it's not. But the thing I've realized as I've gotten older is that your heart has its very own lost-and-found department. Some of the things you've lost forever can be regained in a new form, like trust, but some things you must accept as gone for good, like maybe your gullibility, which is a good thing."

Kendall sat on the edge of the master berth, her legs dangling over the side as she pulled on some footies. "God, my toes are freezing in here," she exclaimed. "I know it's hard to imagine, but someday James will be nothing more than a missing sock to you!"

Katie finally managed to giggle. "Then I'd rather go barefoot."

"Honey," Kendall added gently, "what I see is someone who is stuck. You're afraid to make a move for fear of being wrong again."

"What if I'm broken?" Katie said softly, as if saying the words could make it true. "I want more than anything to move on from my last marriage and not be a damaged, guarded person. But I can't do that without opening myself up to the possibilities. I want to trust again, but it goes beyond trusting him. I don't even know what to pray for because I don't trust in my own ability to make the right choices. I don't trust myself."

"Don't pray for something external. Just pray for your healing," Kendall said. "The further you get from the pain, the more your thoughts redirect to a new place. And that old pain becomes like scar tissue. You get stronger in that area."

Kendall got back under the covers, and Katie mulled over Kendall's words. She thought she'd fallen asleep when she heard Kendall cackle, wide awake again.

"There's this nautical saying I really like. I don't know who it's attributed to, but it goes, 'Give *wine* and tide a chance to change.' You gotta love it when you can blend wine and water wisdom!"

Katie smiled, stifling a laugh. "I think it's *wind*, not *wine*," she said teasingly. "Like sailboats, not powerboats . . . and definitely not *wine*. Sorry to burst your bubble."

When Kendall didn't respond, Katie babbled on. "But they didn't have powerboats when that quote was written."

A few minutes later, she heard her friend's slow, heavy breaths.

Katie focused on the sounds of the water gently caressing the hull, like a light drumbeat marking the slightest movements toward a new tide, a new day. She'd come a long way from the nights she'd fallen asleep on James's musty old yacht, the *Cake & Eat It 2*. In the glistening harbor in sunny Fort Lauderdale, she'd been a married woman who had never felt more alone in her life.

Kendall was right. She was different inside, and that difference was becoming her power. No matter how bad she felt about Deke, or anything, she would never feel that abject sense of isolation anymore.

Is it too late to open my heart to Deke?

Katie tried to find comfort in the blanket of darkness and her new friend's words. Deke had issued a sort of ultimatum, but it wasn't an end. She couldn't imagine the two of them living in the same time zone or hemisphere, let alone the same little town, and not ending up in each other's arms. In the past year, she had found her ground amid the constant flow of life, like a lighthouse within herself. And now, from those banks, she could take risks . . . as long as she didn't lose sight of her own light.

CHAPTER 15

STOWAWAY SANTA

At 0900 hours, Katie paced the dock, repeatedly checking her watch. She had gone into town to help Belle put out their batches of cookies for the first day of HolidayFest, and when she had returned, Kendall was gone. They needed to leave the slip in forty-five minutes for the fifteen-minute journey upriver. Katie was still nervous about leaving the boat unguarded and expected to see Kendall at the helm warming up the engines by then. Instead, she saw a man in a red suit and red hat sitting in the cockpit, his eyes closed and head bent over.

"Thank goodness you're here," Katie said brightly.

Santa's head jerked back with a huge snort, and Katie laughed.

"Sleeping on the job already? I guess you've been busy at the North Pole making all those presents." She expected Santa to pick up on her joke, but he stared at her as if she spoke a foreign language. "You must be Herb," Katie said. "It's nice to meet you."

She was relieved at least Santa was on time, although he seemed a little unsure of what he was doing there. As Katie boarded, Santa stood up shakily, reaching forward to take her hand and nearly tripping over his big black boots. He grabbed for the handrail near the cockpit sink as if he didn't have his sea legs.

"Yo, ho, ho, it's Santa to you, little lady," the man said with a wink, suddenly remembering to get into character.

Herb, er, Santa, was thinner than Katie had imagined, but from a distance, he should look the part, she thought. If he was wearing a wig, it was a good one, and his fake beard and mustache were a good match. Katie wondered if Santa had started a little early on the eggnog, however.

"I think it's 'ho ho ho,' unless you're Pirate Santa. Can I get you some coffee?" she asked.

Santa nodded, apparently a man of few words.

As Katie brewed a fresh pot of coffee in the cabin, she felt the boat move and heard Kendall's voice welcoming their North Pole guest and explaining that he would sit in the big chair secured on the bow. Then, taking her place at the helm, she started the engines and watched the gauges as they warmed up to operating temperature.

Katie came topside with a large coffee for Santa and an insulated Captain mug for Kendall, who tapped it against Katie's First Mate mug. Then she gave a red-and-white Santa hat to Kendall and put one on over her long blonde hair. Gold letters spelled out "Nice" on her hat, while Kendall's hat said "Naughty."

Kendall looked at hers, grinned, and then pulled it down

over her ears. "Cute! I can't wait until Cole sees this. He'll help us secure the boat on the other end."

It was a chilly morning on the first weekend of December, and Katie had paired her hat with a festive neck scarf with colorful hibiscus, something she'd picked up when she'd lived in Florida. Miranda had helped her sew white fur to the collars, wrists, and hem of a one-piece red dress, which she wore with red leggings and black knee-length boots.

"Don't you look the part, Mrs. Claus!" Kendall gawked at Katie's outfit. "Check out your wife, Santa."

Fortunately, he seemed to miss their husband-wife connection.

"Okay, Santa," Katie said, "let's get you situated on the bow. Then we'll stow some presents around you."

Santa strained to stand, and as Katie pulled him up off the bench, he lunged unsteadily toward Kendall, who backed away in disgust. Katie helped him up the steps and stayed close at hand as he plopped himself into the chair with a groan. She looked down at Kendall and rolled her eyes.

Back in the cockpit, Kendall said, "Wouldn't ya know, of all the Santas on the Potomac, we get the one with a drinking problem."

"All he has to do is wave," Katie said, crossing her fingers he wouldn't fall asleep. "He's already got the 'ho ho ho' part down. I checked."

The marine radio crackled, and Kendall switched to channel seventy-two to communicate with the other boaters. "Parade boaters, this is *Char-Don-Eh* at Belmont Bay Marina. Santa has arrived from the North Pole and is onboard. Please confirm readiness for departure when I call out your boat name."

Kendall read from a list of names on her phone.

"*High Cotton?*"

"*High Cotton* ready to roll, Captain."

"*Charge It?*"

"*Charge It* all charged up, Captain."

"*The Rodfather?*"

"Aye, aye. This is the *Rodfather* geared for escort."

After the remaining police and wildlife boats confirmed their vessel numbers, Kendall put the boat into gear and maneuvered the Chris-Craft out of the slip and into the river. Despite the cold, they were blessed with a bright blue sky and high wispy cirrus clouds with a light breeze that made the festive garlands glisten in the sunshine. The recreational boats took the lead, with *Char-Don-Eh* in the middle, followed by the fireboat, unofficially dubbed *Flame Catcher*.

"Mom! Mom!"

A shout on shore caught Katie's attention. Belle was running along the path between the marina and the science center, her long dark hair blowing behind her. She smiled and waved, and Katie waved back and blew kisses. Belle looked like a gangly teen again in a long green-and-red stocking hat with a tassel at the end, and Katie felt a pang at the thought of saying goodbye to her next month. She watched through binoculars as Belle got in the Jeep and sped up the street. She couldn't wipe the smile off her face. Her daughter had made the effort to give them a sendoff and was going to meet them in town with the Beach Bonfire Babes.

Katie queued up the stereo system, and the familiar notes of "Here Comes Santa Claus" accompanied them as they traveled at no-wake speed. Santa's head bobbed with the tune as one black boot tapped to the music. She breathed a sigh of relief. The plan had come together after all.

Santa's floating entourage passed the Potomac Science Center, and Katie focused her binoculars on the boarding platform where she had dropped off Deke on so many occasions. Over the course of the summer and fall, their quick rendezvous at the dock had become prolonged, earnest kisses while she idled the boat in the shallows. She wasn't used to being loved by a man who wasn't expecting, or even demanding, something from her. He seemed to only want her to bring her full self to every moment. It was oddly freeing and slightly unnerving in its lack of possessiveness. She could have more of those tender kisses and so much else. She had opened her heart to life on the Potomac shores.

If only I can open my heart to love . . .

Katie wondered if someone could give a person the space they needed without growing distant. At the same time, maybe togetherness wasn't the penultimate goal. She liked her own time too. Maybe true companionship was about making room for individual interests and needs so personal growth wasn't stifled. No matter how far true friends went, the connection was always there. Even to Texas . . . or the Galapagos.

Have I always known this, or am I learning this for the first time?

They cruised under the Route 1 bridge and the railroad trestle bridge that still carried Amtrak trains up and down the East Coast. After passing rows of covered slips at two marinas on the starboard side, the shoreline became a steep, wooded incline edged by boulders. A lone fishing boat trolled for bass and catfish in the deeper water along the northern bank. On the port side, the captain of the barge at the Vulcan sand yard blew his horn. Patrons at the Harbour Grille lined the dock, their small children jumping up and down at the sight of Santa. At the apartment complex behind the restaurant, people stood on the roof, taking pictures and videos.

Santa waved broadly from his throne and put on a good show, occasionally picking up a wrapped box and shaking it as if to check its belongings. Katie gave a thumbs-up to Kendall, who tooted the boat horn as they passed under the highway bridge and into the last stretch of their journey. The excitement of the crowd at the restaurant was just a taste of what awaited them in town.

Katie was still smiling when she felt her phone buzz in her pocket. Taking off a glove to activate her screen, she quickly glanced at her messages, expecting one from Belle to tell her she'd met up with the Beach Bonfire Babes. But it was a message from Officer Kessler—Randy.

"Glad you found a replacement Santa," the text said. *"I didn't know Herb had COVID."*

Katie looked back at the DWR boat trailing them, then up at Santa on the bow, just as the music switched to a popular hip-hop Christmas song. Santa stood up and started dancing, and Kendall and Katie did a doubletake. Before they could stop him, Santa did a spin in his boots, leaving black marks on the hull.

"Oh no," Kendall mouthed.

Katie couldn't hear her over the sound of the music, so she leaned in, cupping her hand and speaking directly into Kendall's ear. "I think we have a problem. That isn't Herb."

"What?!" Kendall looked at her wide-eyed. "Then who is it?" she yelled, a hint of panic in her voice.

She throttled back to idle, the boat floating slowly forward, and shut off the music. "Bow dancing is not allowed. Please take your seat," Kendall commanded.

Katie responded to Randy on her phone: *"We may have a problem."*

The situation was quickly turning unsafe and chaotic as Santa turned around, beckoning Kendall to join him. "Come on, Captain, let's have a little fun!"

He pulled off his Santa hat and started waving it in the air. Without the hat, which was attached to the beard, his face was fully exposed. The man looked to be about sixty, with a high forehead, dark eyebrows, a salt-and-pepper five o'clock shadow, and platinum white hair that was clearly a bad dye job from a box. His startlingly blue eyes were locked on Kendall.

"Surprise, babe."

Kendall yelled, "Larry, what the—"

That expression explained why Larry had been hard to let go of, Katie thought. He'd mastered the come-hither look, and as he gyrated his hips, Santa started to resemble a dirty old man. Katie half expected Larry to throw Kendall over his shoulder and take her into the cabin. Maybe even willingly.

"Oh shit," Kendall said, just as Santa took a couple steps back, tripping over a present and grabbing at the bow rail.

The next sound was a big splash.

"Santa overboard!" Katie shouted.

"Get me outta here! Get me outta here!" Larry's arms flailed as he tried to tread water in his sopping Santa suit. His head bobbed under the surface, and then he popped back up as the other boats slowed and circled back.

Kendall yelled, "Take off your boots, or you're gonna be an anchor!" Out of earshot, she stifled a laugh and said, "I know this is serious, but it's still kinda funny. Am I wrong?"

Katie ran for the life ring and tossed it into the water with the deftness of a baseball pitcher, striking Larry in the head with the foam ring.

"Oopsy," she said. "And no, you're not wrong."

They watched as Larry grabbed the life ring. The fireboat approached and swung around so the back of it faced Larry. One of the rescue personnel stood on the swim platform and lowered the boarding ladder into the water. He seemed poised to dive in but thought better of it and threw a chunky yellow life jacket into the water.

"Put that over your head and through one arm," he instructed.

He then tossed a line to Larry, who caught it on the third try, and they pulled him toward the boat. Larry looked like a drowned rat as they hoisted him onboard.

Kendall was bent over the steering wheel, tears streaming down her face.

"Are you okay?" Katie was genuinely worried about her friend, until she realized Kendall was laughing uncontrollably.

"Stop it," Katie said, sounding like a petulant toddler. "It's not funny. Now what I am going to do? The HolidayFest is ruined!"

No one was turning out to be dependable, and Katie could barely decide whether to scream or cry. She went into the cabin below, dug her cell phone out of her pocket again, and dialed Chaya, who answered on the first ring and started speaking without any formalities.

"Hey, what's the holdup? Someone heard on the police scanner that there was a water rescue. Please don't tell me someone fell in."

"Yes, not just 'someone,' Chaya. But do not react to this. Do you understand? I don't want anyone to overhear you."

"Oh, no. Okay. Who?" she asked.

"*Santa* fell overboard. He was a stowaway, not the real Santa. It was Loser Larry. He somehow got onboard and put on the costume this morning. We didn't realize until it was too late."

"Oh. My. Gosh. So, where's the costume?"

"The Santa costume? It's on Larry, of course, and he's on the rescue boat. They took him to shore at the closest marina and probably to urgent care, although he belongs back in jail. He's a nuisance to society!"

"Okay, okay, let's focus on solutions for a minute instead of Waterlogged Larry. We need his costume or *a* costume . . . and a man with a beer belly," Chaya said. "The mayor just announced a delay on the loudspeaker, and the oom-pah band near the gazebo is starting up again. He bought you some time."

"I'm clear out of solutions, Chaya. I wanted this to be a magical day—"

"Yeah, yeah, in a magical month, in a magical season, but get a grip. Maybe *you* need some eggnog! Let me see what I can do." Chaya hung up abruptly.

CHAPTER 16

I SAW MOMMY KISSING SANTA CLAUS

The five boats idled in front of the island that divided the river between Prince William Marina and Occoquan Regional Park less than a half mile from the town, waiting for a solution. Katie hoped the real story wasn't already making the rounds. That Santa had gone swimming.

"What's the plan?" Kendall asked, trying to hide a smirk.

"Shut up. I can see you're about to laugh again," Katie said, pointing a gloved finger at her. "You can't even keep a straight face."

Katie knew she was moping, but she couldn't snap out of it. Kendall wasn't helping by not taking the situation seriously.

"I'm sorry," Kendall said, but it was clear she felt more amusement than remorse. "What's the worst that can happen now? Santa shows up by car. Life goes on. I'm freezing my ass off. What are we waiting for?"

"I texted Chaya. She said Plan B is on the way, whatever that is. Keep your eyes peeled."

They both scanned the river but didn't see any boats. Or Santas.

Kendall shook her head. "Geez, why don't they just have Santa drop in from a Coast Guard helicopter? This is starting to feel like a stealth operation."

"It's not like Santas grow on trees," Katie said. "I imagine all the costumes are rented for the season. Maybe they borrowed Santa from the mall for a few hours."

"Well, I gotta use the head. My bladder is too old for this. I'll be right back."

Kendall headed into the cabin while Katie walked over to the transom, just as a man in a red suit climbed aboard from a rowing scull. She watched in amazement as he hauled the small boat onto the swim platform in one swift movement and secured it with bungee cords.

"Ho ho ho, ma'am. Permission to come aboard?" Santa asked in a deep voice, clearly trying to bellow in fake grandfatherly style as he stepped over the transom door. His eyes sparkled a mischievous greenish-blue as he made adjustments to what was obviously a pillow inside his costume. "My apologies, ma'am. I didn't have room for my belly on that little boat."

"Whaaaat?" Kendall shrieked when she came back outside. "Where did you come from?"

"Santa to the rescue," the man said sheepishly. "Were you expecting someone else?"

"He rowed here apparently," Katie said. "We couldn't see him because he was so close to the waterline."

Kendall radioed to the adjacent boats to get in formation, and Katie called Chaya.

"Santa's here. Can you tell the mayor we're continuing the parade? We should be there in under ten minutes."

"Aye, aye, Miss Claus," teased Chaya.

"Whatever," Katie said, tired of all the jokes. "Let's get this show on the road."

The new-and-improved Santa, who was very steady on his long legs, took his spot in the chair on the bow. He was missing the black boots, but his red sneakers blended in with the costume. And he'd even brought a kid's fishing pole, the kind with a colorful wand and a piece of rope dangling from it. At the end of the line, the fake fishhook had been replaced by a plastic ball of mistletoe. Nice touch, Santa. Wherever they had found him, he was a keeper.

Katie turned on the holiday music again as they proceeded upriver and breathed a sigh of relief as they approached the last of the three bridges spanning the Occoquan. Her excitement built when she saw the throng of people lining the town dock, waving and cheering their arrival. As the boat slowed to docking speed, Katie had a vision of her mom bundled up in her long wool coat, a black scarf over her blonde curls, and leaning against the lantern at the end of the boardwalk, just like she used to greet Katie and Belle in the same boat parade years before. The memory was bittersweet, and Katie wiped a tear from her eye as Santa stood up and held out his hand to her.

Kendall shooed her to join him on the bow. "Go on. You pulled this event together," she said. "Enjoy your moment."

"Hey, look, there are my grandsons," Kendall yelled, pointing to two boys in green who looked more like tiny elves. "My daughter made it in time. Oh my God. I'm getting all teary here."

One of the elves was holding something, but it squirmed out of his arms and ran back and forth along the dock like a wind-up toy with a white perm. She watched as Kendall's grandson tried to catch the tiny dog, with Cole close on their heels.

"And Frosty," Kendall cooed.

From the bow, Katie could see Belle and the Beach Bonfire Babes lined up near Bonfire Voices, each holding one of Miranda's bells and ringing it wildly. She could just hear the trilling of the bells over the sound of "I Saw Mommy Kissing Santa Claus."

Santa raised his fishing pole, the mistletoe dangling like a flowery lure, and stepped closer to her. "So, you've been *nice* this year?" he asked.

"Huh?" Katie tried to take a step back but bumped into the artificial fireplace.

Santa pointed to the words stenciled on her hat.

"Oh." She giggled. "I hope so."

"Oh, I know so," Santa said.

Before she could object, he put his arm around her waist, pulling her even closer against his protruding belly, and bent her backwards. At first, she thought he was attempting a smooth dance step in sync with the song.

Boy, this Santa's got some moves.

Then wide-eyed, she noticed the mistletoe dangling over her head, just as Santa leaned forward and laid a big kiss on her gaping mouth. She gripped his surprisingly muscular arms and tried to extract herself without causing a scene, but the pressure of his mouth on hers was relentless. Exquisitely relentless.

Time stood still as she floated ever so slowly toward the dock in Santa's arms. Even through the red suit and beard, he smelled like a Yankee Candle, a familiar blend of mahogany and teakwood, and his lips were warm and soft. So warm and so soft.

Why do I want to kiss him back?

"Hey, hey, knock it off, lovebirds."

Katie recognized Chaya's voice from the shore.

"I'm trying to dock here, guys," Kendall yelled.

Santa finally pulled away, and Katie straightened, adjusting her hat and dress and waving at the clapping crowd as if they had rehearsed that move. She was in love with Deke, but she'd just let jolly old St. Nick kiss her. Kinda sorta. And she had a feeling she would have enjoyed kissing him back. In fact, she felt like she knew him, and she worried that Stowaway Santa had found his way back onboard.

"Who do you think you are?" she said through her smile, trying to make it clear kissing strangers wasn't part of her holiday repertoire while keeping up the act. When she saw the twinkle in his eye, she feigned outrage and yanked his beard. The hat and beard came off in her hands, but the mustache remained. She pinched it between her fingers and yanked again.

"Hey," Santa yelped. He stepped back, mustache still intact. It was the softest mustache she had ever touched. The only mustache she had ever touched.

Before Katie could fully register what was happening, or who Santa really was, he tripped over a present. She watched helplessly as his red sneakers danced across the bow, and he grabbed at the rail. She reached for the plastic fishing pole, trying to find a way to stop his momentum, but it snapped as he started to fall.

"Oh, no! Deke!"

The next sound was another big splash, followed by another yelp of pain.

CHAPTER 17

HOME FOR THE HOLIDAYS

Katie maneuvered the wheelchair along walkways lined with evergreens that represented every US state, territory, and the District of Columbia, hunting for the Georgia and Virginia trees as they explored the Pathway of Peace at the Ellipse near the National Mall. In the center, a tree nearly thirty feet tall stood like a beacon of light over President's Park between the White House and the Washington Monument.

"I can't believe I've never been here before," Deke said. "It's interesting to see how each state decorates its tree with things unique to that state."

Katie had been coming to the Pageant of Peace as long as she could remember, long before Belle was born, when she was a child herself. She was excited to show everyone the historic holiday landmark in Washington started by President and First Lady Coolidge nearly a hundred years earlier.

"Back in the 1950s," she said, "they pumped in artificial snow and had a live Nativity scene. The sheep got out and

~ 137 ~

were running around in rush-hour traffic. And Santa used to arrive on a sleigh drawn by reindeer. That was before my time, but Mom and Dad told us about it."

She stopped at the giant Yule log pit, and Deke pulled her into his lap while they waited for Chaya and Danylo, who were checking out the Hanukkah display during the Festival of Lights. It was the last night of Hanukkah, and all nine candles were lit on the thirty-foot gold menorah.

Kendall, her daughter Alexis, and her grandsons had run ahead to look at the live donkeys and reindeer. Alexis was only a few years older than Belle, and Belle enjoyed playing with her boys.

Katie watched the huge logs spit and crackle in the large pit covered with steel grates. "In medieval times, they would light the Yule log on Christmas Eve and keep it burning through the twelve days of Christmas," she said. "They kept a small fragment to ward off evil spirits throughout the year and used it to light the next year's Yule log."

"Wow, now who's the walking Wikipedia?" Deke chuckled. "You're like a Christmas historian."

"It's my favorite holiday. What can I say? But enough with my old stories. How was the orthopedist?"

After Secret Santa fell overboard, Deke could no longer access his third-floor walkup apartment. The fall had hyperextended one of his knees, resulting in a stretched ligament, a posterior cruciate ligament injury, and he would be on crutches through the holidays. Katie invited him to move into the guest room at the river house until he could handle stairs again. The wheelchair was useful for public outings, and Cole had built a temporary wheelchair ramp over the few front steps to the porch. Thankfully, the PCL injury didn't require surgery, and Deke had just started physical therapy that day.

"How long did he say you needed to be off your leg?" Katie asked.

Deke nuzzled his face into her long hair. "Two to three orgasms."

"Shush. Someone might hear you." Katie giggled.

"Okay. Two to three months, but two orgasms a day."

"Uh-huh, good luck with that," she teased. "Besides, we still have to behave."

"I know, I know, but what's a little knee pain when I get to live with you and Belle in your Christmas wonderland? And focus on what's really important in life."

"Well, I'm just sorry you—"

"If you say you're sorry one more time," Deke admonished, "I'm going to move in permanently and never leave. It was just my way of getting a hall pass to your bedroom every night. Well, if I could walk down the hall."

Katie shook her head and hugged him. "And it was worth getting stuck in immigration in a developing country? I still can't believe you got that far with an expired passport. You took me completely by surprise."

Deke pursed his lips. "Well, that's not *exactly* how it happened."

Katie touched his mustache and looked into his eyes. "What do you mean?"

"It was an easy explanation for our friends, but in truth, my passport was fine. My heart just wasn't into the project." He gazed into the glowing fire. "I wanted to be here, to experience all of this with you and Belle. When I got to the Darwin Institute, I found out a couple of the regular staff weren't vaccinated, so they weren't cleared to travel home for the holidays. They didn't really need me."

He looked at Katie and touched her cheek. "I was hoping you did."

That night after Belle had gone to bed, Deke asked Katie to bring in a box from his car. She expected another Christmas present to put under the tree, but the unwrapped box was dusty, like it had been in storage for a while, and it had been taped over many times.

"Deke, I still can't believe you're here with me. And at Christmas."

"Well, now that you're stuck with me," he said, "I'm hoping I can share a little piece of my holiday tradition with you. I haven't looked in this box in, gosh, at least fifteen years."

He opened the box and carefully removed balls of crumpled newspaper. He lined up almost twenty individually wrapped items on the table. "This is a Nativity scene my mom painted when I was in elementary school."

He unwrapped each ceramic piece and studied it before handing it to Katie. "I used to line up the camel and the sheep and pretend they were trekking across the desert in search of pyramids," Deke said. "GI Joe was the archaeologist. I was a little confused with my geography and timelines."

"That's adorable. Did GI Joe find frankincense and myrrh in Egypt?" Katie asked.

"Yes. He also found a mummy that turned out to be King Tut. But he didn't find baby Jesus."

Katie laughed and started to arrange the figurines on the mantel, realizing Jesus was the one piece missing from the Nativity scene. "Oh, you weren't kidding," she said. "We have no babe wrapped in swaddling clothes to lie in the manger."

Deke stood up, leaning on a crutch. "I don't know what happened to him, but the crèche looks really beautiful there," he said. "My mom would be so pleased. She appreciated all the little things, the same way you do."

"Like her little boy," Katie said, kissing Deke on the cheek. "But I save too much. Most of the stuff in this house only has meaning to my family, not anyone else. I still can't get the old grandfather clock running again, but it looks pretty anyway."

"Katie, you could adorn your house in famous artwork, and people would ooh and aah and be impressed with your taste. But I put a lot more value in the personal items that have stories behind them, the objects that connect us to the past and the long line of people that came before us. Like the quilts you hung on the walls in the guest room. I feel like I'm sleeping in a roomful of people that made you the woman you are today."

She squeezed his shoulder. "I guess I'm a contemporary archaeologist. I don't dig things out of the ground. I dig them out of my basement and garage."

He chuckled. "There's some truth in that. They're part of your story. And this Nativity scene is part of my story."

"Hold that thought," Katie said. She spent a few minutes rummaging around in the garage and returned with something hidden in her fist. She opened her hand to reveal a figurine of an infant. "My mom's Nativity set was carved out of wood, so it's the best I can do."

Deke put baby Jesus inside the manger, completing the scene, and Katie adjusted the hanging star at the crown of the wooden stable.

"There," she said. "Now there's a part of my story in your story."

CHAPTER 18

TINSEL & TALES

"Here's to our first Occoquan HolidayFest," Katie said, lifting a cranberry-spiced martini garnished with a colorful rim of seasonal spices. The Beach Bonfire Babes gathered in their own gallery, along with their families and significant others, to celebrate their first year in business. They had opened the gallery in May and made it through three seasons.

In a crystal punch bowl, Kendall stirred a festive concoction of cranberry compote and cranberry juice with red cranberries bobbing on top, and Cole dipped each martini glass into a saucer of sugar and spice to form a sweet wreath around the edge. "Naughty or nice?" Kendall asked Chaya, pointing to the bottle of vodka for those who wanted a little more kick. She finished off each drink with an ice cube of crushed pineapple.

Katie approached Chaya, and they moved from drinks to dessert. Belle's enormous display of Christmas cookies looked too good to eat.

"Mom, I made a special Christmas tree cookie for you," Belle said. "It's made the same way as the wreaths, but I changed the design to be our eternal tree. That's why it's got candies in all different colors on it."

The tree looked like it was covered in Skittles, and Katie smiled, remembering the tins of cookies her grandmother would send every Christmas. Belle had baked every cookie in the family recipe collection: German pfeffernuss rolled in powdered sugar, icebox cookies with pecans that looked like sandies, peppermint-frosted candy canes, green wreaths with red cinnamons for berries, bells sprinkled in white sugar with silver candy balls, and sugar cookie stars with blue sprinkles.

"You've outdone yourself this year, babe," Katie said, hugging Belle. "And the bûche de Noël is perfection. I don't know how you roll sponge cake into the shape of a Yule log, but it's truly artistic and perfect for a party at Bonfire Voices."

"I've had years of practice," Belle said, beaming. She loved to bake, and she had been perfecting her chocolate and vanilla buttercream Christmas cake ever since a trip to the Christmas markets in Europe with Katie's mom, who had made her granddaughter her official travel partner after they lost Katie's dad. As a travel agent, Clara had often scouted out new itineraries for her clients, and she brought Belle along during school breaks.

"You're fortunate to have so many great memories with Grandma. Hey, let's keep an eye on the time. I don't want to be late for the ballet," Katie said, and Belle nodded.

"So, have you figured it out?" Chaya asked, stepping closer to Katie.

"Figured what out?" Katie asked, eyeing her friend quizzically. "Why more and more spiders keep hatching in our Christmas tree?" She pointed toward the artificial evergreen, which was now draped in a tinsel-like web. "And all over town, for that matter."

"Ah, that's a story for Danylo to tell," she said, glancing toward him. "But have you figured out how Deke ended up in a Santa suit?"

"Oh, do tell. We've been so busy dealing with his, um, injury that I haven't unraveled how that whole day went down," Katie said.

"Well, my original plan was to have Danylo substitute for Santa after Lockdown Larry fell in the water, but I had to find a costume," explained Chaya. "I ran up and down Mill Street and finally found one at the spa that took over the old Golden Goose. Remember the Christmas shop that was on the corner for like forty years?"

She paused, and Katie nodded.

"The new owners found some old displays in the back, including a Santa mannequin, and they had just put it on their porch step. I asked if I could borrow the costume for a few hours."

Katie nodded again as she nibbled on her gooey Christmas tree, the cornflakes fused together with melted marshmallow. "This would be the perfect Christmas s'more. We should add it to our menu." She licked her fingers and shook her head as she tried to make sense of the story. "But I still don't understand how you knew Deke was back in town."

"He called Danylo from the airport to find out how the parade was going," Chaya explained. "We got his rowing shell ready for him at the dock, and he changed into the costume as soon as the cab dropped him off.”

Katie shook her head in disbelief. “So, you were all in on it.”

“Well, only me and Danylo. Meanwhile, Larry was in the back of an ambulance and the police arrested him. Again.”

“Chaya, thank you for trying so hard. We almost saved Christmas for the little town of Occoquan, if Santa hadn’t gotten a little frisky.” Katie smiled sheepishly at the memory. As much as she had fought the kiss, it had been a nice one.

“Yeah, I didn’t orchestrate that part!” Chaya said. “But all the kids saw Santa from the dock, before he went swimming. We forgot to consider how most kids don’t have the vaccine yet since it just came out last month. They wouldn’t have been able to sit on Santa’s lap anyway. It was safer that way. And a memory they will never forget!”

“Good point.”

Suddenly, all the lights went out in the gallery. There was a collective gasp, then hushed voices as everyone turned their eyes to the tree, which sparkled with the only light in the room. Danylo stood by it and beckoned to Chaya, who glanced at Katie with raised eyebrows and then joined him.

“I want to thank you for welcoming me into your lives this holiday,” Danylo said in his thick Ukrainian accent. “I was worried about taking on this project and feeling alone at a time of year when we want to be with loved ones. I am very lucky to have found this group of friends and,” he paused, glancing at Chaya, “to have met someone who is becoming an important part of my life.”

Katie joined Deke on one of the windowsill benches where he was resting his leg, and he put his arm around her.

"In my country," Danylo continued, "we have a tradition that comes from a Christmas tale." He pointed toward the tree. "You see, a long, long time ago in a little Ukrainian village, a poor woman and her children lived in a small dirt house. The woman had lost her husband and didn't have the means to provide special food or presents for her family at Christmas. But in the center of their little house, a tree had grown in the earthen floor. The children wanted to decorate the tree, but they didn't even have string. It was a sad Christmas Eve, and the children went to bed early, wishing for a magical Christmas morning.

"Meanwhile, a tiny spider watched the family from a corner of the room, feeling sorry for them and wanting to help. During the night, the spider spun a beautiful web all over the bare Christmas tree in the corner. In the morning when the children woke, the spider web sparkled in the sunlight, kind of like your 'tinsel.'"

Danylo removed a spider ornament from the tree and handed it to one of Kendall's grandsons. "Pass this around for everyone to touch," he said. "The spider is called *pavuchky* in my language, and we decorate our trees with these little guys as a reminder that happiness and good fortune can come from the smallest things."

He took Chaya's hand.

"And in the most unexpected ways."

"I love this version," Katie said to Belle as they took their seats in the Warner Theatre in Washington, DC.

The Washington Ballet's rendition of the Tchaikovsky classic *The Nutcracker* was set in Georgetown in the late 1800s, with George Washington as the Nutcracker, King George III as the Rat King, and party guests including Harriet Tubman and Frederick Douglass.

Seeing *The Nutcracker* had been a mother-daughter tradition since Belle had taken ballet as a preschooler. The previous year they had settled for watching it on television. With theaters opening again, she and Belle had opted for seats in one of the boxes in the historic building that dated back to the vaudeville days of the 1920s.

"I love that the little girl's name is Clara, like Grandma," Belle said, and Katie bumped her shoulder, afraid of showing too much affection.

Katie always tried to find the right balance of emotion with her daughter. Sometimes Belle was open to her mother's displays of love, and other times they seemed to backfire. Once Belle had told Katie, "I don't know why, but sometimes you just annoy me for no reason at all." Katie hoped someday Belle would not feel smothered or controlled by her mother's love, but Katie remembered feeling the same way with her own mother, even in what turned out to be her dying days. Katie looked up at the ornate ceiling, wondering if Mom was watching from above, and uttered a silent apology.

The curtain rose with the familiar flutes of the Miniature Overture, and Katie was entranced by the uniquely American version of the ballet. After the clock struck midnight, Act I became a Revolutionary War battle in toe shoes as the Nutcracker came to life as George Washington fighting the red-coated rats with his Valley Forge Bunnies. Deke would love the unique angle of this version, Katie thought, but she reminded herself they would be walking in George Washington's footsteps on Christmas Eve. If only Deke could actually walk.

"I forgot about the cherry blossoms," Belle whispered as the Nutcracker-turned-Prince led Clara to meet the Sugar Plum Fairy in Act II amid the dancing cherry blossoms of Washington in spring.

Katie smiled and instinctively squeezed Belle's hand. She didn't pull away. She held Katie's hand until the last scene when Clara fell asleep with her beloved Nutcracker doll, leaving the audience to wonder if the entire performance of the dancing soldiers, rats, flowers, mushrooms, and more was all just a dream.

"Come on, Mom," Belle said, heading for the aisle as soon as the lights went up.

Katie moved a little slower, still mesmerized by the dreamy performance. "Do you want to go to the Willard for a drink? Or there's a rooftop bar on top of the Hotel Washington right around the corner. I hear it has incredible views."

But Katie sounded a little too earnest, and Belle was back to her twenty-year-old self. Katie knew the magic had been there for a little while, and that would have to be enough.

CHAPTER 19

ALL IS CALM, ALL IS BRIGHT

Deke carefully made his way along the brick sidewalk leading to Pohick Church using a three-footed aluminum cane. He and Katie had arrived early for the Episcopal Christmas Eve service in the hopes of sitting in the pew box once owned by the Washington family, who had lived just seven miles away at Mount Vernon. Washington surveyed Truro Parish in 1767 and lobbied for this spot for Pohick Church. The Washingtons and other wealthy landowners like George Mason and George William Fairfax helped fund the construction of the Georgian-style brick church by purchasing family pews.

As luck would have it, the famous pew box was empty, and they settled in on embroidered cushions. Deke looked around at the raised pulpit in the center of the church and the organ pipes at the back.

"I've got goose bumps sitting here," Deke whispered. Can't you just imagine George and Martha sitting across from us?"

Katie's warm smile masked the shiver she felt as she looked at Deke in his navy-blue suit with a buttoned-down white shirt, gold tie, and wingtip tan shoes. She was relieved to see he was able to put more pressure on his knee, and there wouldn't be any permanent damage. Belle had attended the family service earlier with friends she had known since her Sunday school classes at the church, but Katie preferred the midnight candlelight service.

The choir and brass quartet opened with "O Come All Ye Faithful." Katie looked up at the cross carved from a walnut tree at Mount Vernon and the graffiti from when the church was occupied by troops from both sides during the Civil War. She closed her eyes and imagined the horses that once milled between the aisles when the church was used as a stable by Union forces.

Just like in her home, Katie drew strength from the connections to the past, the people whose perseverance left remnants of a harder time. When the soloist began to sing "Silent Night" in German, just as it was performed in Austria in 1818, she touched her lighted candle to Deke's and met his gaze in the dim, flickering light, one damaged heart to another.

"All is calm, all is bright," she sang softly, looking forward to the coming year.

On Christmas morning, Katie found Deke sitting in front of the fireplace with Maui and Kauai lying on the hearth. The first rays of sunlight found their way through the treetops and into the tall windows of the river room, and a mist rose from Belmont Bay like the cloak of winter.

"Can I make some coffee?" Katie asked. She knew Belle wouldn't be up for another hour or two, and she looked forward to the quiet time to exchange presents with Deke. She had prepared a breakfast casserole the day before and turned on the oven to preheat.

"I brewed a pot already, hon. Get a cup and come join me. I need you to sit right here," he said, patting the sofa. "C'mon, it's almost seven."

Katie noticed an envelope on the coffee table. She grabbed Deke's presents from under the tree and set them in front of him.

"What's important about seven a.m.?" Katie asked. "Am I forgetting something?"

He smiled, watching her face, just as the foyer was filled with loud, lyrical chimes that resounded throughout the two-story great room.

"Is someone here? Santa's ringing the doorbell?" she asked, mystified by the long sequence of the Westminster melody, which was followed by seven distinctive gongs counting out the hour. "Oh, Deke. You didn't."

Katie couldn't hide the overwhelming emotion. She jumped up and ran over to the grandfather clock, where the pendulum swung, and new brass chains glittered in the glass case. "You fixed the grandfather clock?"

She ran back to him in her robe and slippers and wrapped her arms around him, kissing him on the cheek. "I haven't heard that sound since my dad died. He always maintained the clock, and Mom didn't know how to keep it going . . . or didn't want to. I can't believe you—" She was so moved, she could barely speak.

"I can't believe you didn't notice the pendulum moving sooner," Deke said. "The horologist came out earlier in the week to replace the old, rusted machinery, but I've had the sound turned off until this morning. There's a switch that controls it. We need to remember to keep everything oiled from now on."

Katie shook her head, amazed he was even aware of the silent clock and took the time to arrange the repair. "*Horologist*, huh? No wonder I didn't know who to call. I can't thank you enough," she said, taking a sip of her coffee. "Okay, it's your turn."

With Deke's eclectic interests, Katie felt she had found the perfect gifts for him, a smart bird feeder with a built-in camera to take bird selfies and a wooden bowl from the shops at Mount Vernon.

"Wow, I can attach this feeder to my balcony rail, or if you don't mind, I can keep it here where you probably get a wider variety of birds," he said. "I can watch the app on my phone, so it almost doesn't matter where the feeder is."

"Sure, I'd love that." His smoker had already taken up a semi-permanent space on her balcony as had his telescope. She liked the idea of mingling Deke's things with hers.

When he opened the bowl, he ran his hands over its raw edges. "This is so unusual," he said, "the way the woodturner didn't smooth out the rim of the bowl."

"Let me explain," Katie said. "That piece of wood you're holding is from a historic white oak that fell on the grounds of Mount Vernon. They used tree ring dating—"

"Dendrochronology," Deke interjected.

"Right, to date the tree to about 1706. They made these beautiful bowls out of the wood."

"Wow, that's incredible," Deke said. "George Washington must have passed this tree on his walks. I'd love to see the exact spot where the tree lived."

He slowly ran a hand over the inside of the bowl and then looked at Katie with a serious expression, his eyes welling up. "This is the . . . best . . . gift. You know me so well."

"Um, you can keep that here too, if you'd like," she teased, trying to lighten the moment, and he laughed.

"Okay, now it's your turn," Deke said. He handed the legal-size envelope to her. Then, with a mischievous look, he reached underneath the sofa pillow and pulled out a Christmas stocking. "This is from your Secret Santa. Look in the stocking first."

Katie grinned and reached her hand deep into the stocking. She felt something soft and plush and pulled it out, studying its black and white markings and long black bill.

"Aww, it's a, well, I was gonna say a penguin, but it's kinda small. A puffin?" she asked.

"You had it right the first time," Deke said. "Penguins mate for life, by the way." He winked at her. "Okay, keep going."

The next stuffed animal she removed from the stocking was a bird resembling a seagull but with bright blue feet. "Wait, I definitely know this one," Katie said. "Aren't they called blue-footed boobies?"

"Yes, that's right. Very good. There might be a theme here," he said.

"A theme, hmmm, like water birds maybe? Is a penguin a bird or a mammal?"

"Penguins are flightless birds," he confirmed. "But there's something else in there."

Katie reached down to the tip of the stocking. The next stuffed animal was a yellow bird.

"Oh, it's a goldfinch, like the ones on my mom's finch feeder. They were her favorites. You know, that's why she named her Jeep 'Yellowbird,' right?" She was so excited about identifying each bird correctly, she didn't stop to wonder why he was giving her a stuffed animal collection.

"Okay. The finch is not the correct replica, but it was as close as I could get. You can learn the difference between your finches when we get there," he said, handing her the envelope.

"When we get where?" Katie's face twisted as she tried to figure out where the gift was going and slowly ran her finger under the sealed flap of the envelope. She glanced at him and frowned. "This better not be another index card."

"Can you think of a place where penguins, blue-footed boobies, and finches all live together?" he asked. "Think of your dog's name."

"Darwin?"

With that, the Old English sheepdog bounded into the room, followed on his heels by Brigid. Both dogs jumped on the sofa, sniffing at the presents excitedly until Brigid seized the penguin in her mouth and ran off, Darwin in hot pursuit.

Deke shook his head. "I'm not going to be able to get that away from her right now. Let's try to focus on the continuity of the gifts, okay?"

"Got it. Odd birds. Oh, and you must mean the scientist Darwin," she whispered so the dogs wouldn't hear. "And . . ."

Katie gingerly opened the envelope as she replayed some of their conversations in her head, particularly the ones about the evolution of species. Recognition dawned on her as she removed a piece of paper from the envelope with an itinerary.

"Deke, you can't be serious. This is a trip to the Galapagos."

"I just can't imagine going there alone now," he said, his voice wavering as if unsure what she would say. "I wanted to take you on this trip, but the timing wasn't right for you."

His words came out in a rush. "We can snorkel with sea lions that come right up to you because they never learned to be afraid of predators. And I'll show you the finches. If Darwin hadn't been terribly seasick, he may never have deduced the theory of natural selection—survival of the fittest. He hated being on the boat, so he spent a lot of time on land observing the differences in the finch beaks from one island to the next and realized, with all other things being equal in the environment, the finches had evolved unique characteristics to capture the available food sources."

He took her face in his hands. "Katie, it's the most amazing place on earth, and I just have to see your eyes light up when you see it," he said emphatically. "It hit me like a ton of bricks on the way there. Now that I love you, I want to share everything I love with you. I want to be more than a scientific observer. I want to be a participant in the world. With you."

"This is so incredibly generous, Deke," she said, tears streaming down her face. "My heart is bursting."

And my heart is healing.

The heaviness that had plagued Katie for the past year finally felt less like brokenness and more like wholeness. She wasn't the same Katie anymore, but the new version understood the motivations that had led her to make the naive choices she had made in the past. In loving Deke, she was only motivated by one thing, and it wasn't to check a box or answer a ticking clock or fill a void. It was simply to love *this* man, to match the love he offered with the same fierce faith, love, and finally, trust.

He brushed her tears away with his thumbs and kissed her.

"We've only just begun," he said.

EPILOGUE

"**M**ore surprises? I don't think you can top the last one," Katie said to Deke as he gingerly made his way toward the boat dock at the Potomac Science Center on crutches. The *Sea Bug,* the small research boat, was already cleated to the floating boarding platform.

"When and how did you put the boat in the water?" She knew he had to trailer it to the boat ramp to use it.

"I have a TA this semester," Deke said, "and he's in charge of taking water samples."

"On Christmas Day?" Katie asked.

"Yep. He didn't go home for the holidays. But stop asking so many questions," Deke said. "I know what you're trying to do, Katydid, and I'm not going to tell you where we're going."

Katie untied the lines and stepped aboard. "Are you sure this is a good idea in your, uh, condition?"

He pulled his red wool cap down over his ears, pretending to tune her out as he shifted the boat into gear.

Although it was midafternoon, presumably the warmest part of the day, the temperatures were still in the mid-thirties. Katie knew it would be at least ten degrees colder on the water, but she had never been just a fair-weather boater. As the buildings and townhomes along the shoreline got smaller and smaller, Katie felt a sense of peace overtake her. The water was a gunmetal gray, and the sky just a lighter shade of gray, but small patches of baby-blue peeked out from the low cloud cover with a hint of optimism, as if the planet was in on Deke's secret, waiting to reveal it.

He brought the boat up on plane as they left the no-wake zone. Katie felt the bow lift gently off the water, and tears streamed from her eyes in the biting breeze. She adjusted her neck gaiter to cover her nose and mouth.

Deke yelled over the sound of the wind and engine, "You doin' okay up there?"

She gave him a thumbs-up sign since he couldn't see her broad smile. She watched as mallards took off in the shallows near the Occoquan Bay National Wildlife Refuge, disturbed by their wake. The ducks skimmed the surface, crossing behind them and landing in the water near a downed tree.

Deke made a sharp turn to port and steered the boat into Belmont Bay, passing the point where they'd rescued Kendall little more than a month before. Katie fondly remembered the night of the full moon. They'd come so far in their relationship since that evening, the exploration and uncertainty replaced by a growing familiarity with each other and confidence in their commitment. Being naked in Deke's arms was as peaceful and fulfilling as a day on the water. She could be wholly in the moment, abandoning her insecurities and riding the intense wave of desire they generated when they touched.

On their starboard side, the sandy shoreline rose to the sandstone bluffs of Mason Neck State Park. Katie looked to her left at the wooded ridge on the opposite side of the bay. The red roof of Bonnie Brae was easy to spot above the leafless trees, and she said a silent prayer of thanks for the blessings of the past year. She'd resolved the land dispute, put her mother's ashes to rest, and taken over the property as her own with the help of her brother. Although the adjacent lot was still barren, she imagined the rows of vines that would take over the hillside in the next few years as a way to stabilize the erosion.

At the water's edge, it was harder to imagine a new dock and boathouse. That dream seemed farther afield simply because it was closer to her heart. But with every passing day, she got closer to her captain's license and the delivery of her new boat.

Give wind and tide a chance to change, Katie.

Deke throttled back, bringing the boat off plane as they reached the east side of the bay where Kane's Creek led into the Great Marsh. The tidal creek meandered into the protected area and was navigable for about a mile at high tide with a shallow-draft boat.

Earlier that year during the cicada emergence, Deke and Katie had come up the creek to record the mating calls of the periodical insects. She wondered what he planned to show her there in the dead of winter. The state park bordered the first refuge established to protect nesting bald eagles, and

Katie knew the eagles would be active in mating season. It was also one of the largest great blue heron rookeries in Virginia, and she noticed the tall bird wading in the shallows.

"Look," Deke whispered, pointing toward a whitetail deer standing at the edge of a hiking trail.

Katie rose and stood next to Deke at the helm. She uncovered her face and smiled up at him as he pulled her close with his free arm. Ahead of them in the brown reeds along the shoreline, Katie noticed white bodies bobbing in the shallows, little white tails tipped up to the bluer sky. She was used to seeing colorful waterfowl in iridescent shades of green and blue, but the birds were much bigger than the white seagulls that frequented the Occoquan River.

Deke put the boat in neutral and, as they coasted closer to the large, elegant birds, he shut off the engine entirely and put a paddle over the side to guide the boat's drift. When a bird bobbed up next to them, Katie gasped at the long, graceful neck and black beak.

Wide-eyed, she whispered, "The tundra swans are here."

Tears streamed down her face as she gaped at the stunning beauty around them. The birds foraged in the shallows, and their high-pitched *woo-hoo* sounds surrounded them, the only other noise the water lapping the hull.

"I've only heard of them. I've never seen them," Deke said softly.

"Same," Katie said, beaming. She rested her head on Deke's chest, her arms wrapped around his waist.

"They fly thirty-seven-hundred miles at fifty miles an hour just to come here to this spot on Belmont Bay," Deke said incredulously. "They probably flew right over your house and waved to you with their big white wings."

"Can you imagine? Their idea of summer vacation is to leave the Arctic tundra and come right here to our backyard," Katie said. "Of all the places on earth they could go, they pick our little piece of paradise."

Deke reached into his pocket and pulled out an index card. Katie frowned and rolled her eyes when she saw it in his hand.

"Oh, no. Now what?"

He faced her with a grin on his face. "I did a little research about tundra swans, that's all," he said, glancing at the card. "Do you know they actually 'date'?"

"What on earth do you mean?" Katie asked.

"It's kind of unusual. A tundra swan pair will spend almost a year together before mating, and then they breed for life." Deke winked at her. "During breeding season, the mated pair will live completely alone for months, fiercely protecting their nests, just the two of them and the families they create."

"That's beautiful," Katie said, just as a bevy of swans ran across the water's surface and then rose in flight, their long necks outstretched.

Their wings made a whistling sound as they circled and flew deeper into the marsh.

"They're like snow angels," she said. "Look at how they glide."

"They have five-foot wing spans and fly as high as nine-thousand feet," Deke continued. "And they navigate using the Earth's magnetic field."

"That's some pretty powerful magnetism," Katie said, poking Deke in the ribs.

"It sure is," he said knowingly. "They never get off course, and they always find their way home."

End

A NEW YEAR'S RESOLUTION
FROM THE AUTHOR

Dear Reader,

Thank you for reading *Santa Overboard*, the first holiday adventure in the Potomac Shores series and a fun story to write after introducing Katie and the Beach Bonfire Babes in *The Cicada Spring*. I love receiving feedback from my readers, talking to you in person at book events, hearing from you through the contact form on my website or on social media, wherever we cross paths. I read all my reviews, and it warms my heart when you feel a connection with my characters, storylines, or setting.

For many authors, the joy of crafting stories is overshadowed by the challenge of building a presence through marketing and publicity to get our books noticed. With the help of my writing community, I am launching a movement called **Review It Forward** to encourage readers to develop a reviewer habit. Reviews are a significant part of determining book rankings in online bookstores and in search engines. Similar to leaving a tip for good service, a thoughtful reader review can go a long way in an author's daily efforts to give life to a book and to help sustain a career as a writer.

It seems only fitting to include my New Year's resolution in my first book focused on the holiday season, and my resolution for 2025 is to always leave a constructive review when I finish reading a book. Even if the story isn't my cup of tea, I will always reward effort over outcome and consider the blood, sweat, and tears that go into every word and thought shared by an author. Many authors are writing in every spare moment they can find, and every little bit of support helps. Leaving a review is free, and your support through your thoughtful assessment is an investment in the future of the written word. I urge you to commit to the same resolution in 2025 and beyond to make reviewing part of your reading habit. Review It Forward!

With best wishes for a blessed holiday season, and happy reading, Carolyn

ACKNOWLEDGMENTS

My biggest struggle in writing this short novel was conjuring up a sense of holiday spirit in the springtime, amid budding trees and crocuses shooting up in the flower beds in Virginia. I had just started a master's degree program in fiction writing at Lindenwood University, and I was juggling writing with classwork, even workshopping some of the scenes in my classes. Along the way, I felt like the universe (or my mother) was giving me signs to keep going. One day, I discovered a brooch in my mother's jewelry box, one I had never noticed before—a cobweb with a tiny spider on it. *Keep going,* it said. My ancestors are from Germany on my mother's side, and the tale of the Christmas spider is also found in German legend.

Another day, still trying to channel Thanksgiving and Christmas as the tulips bloomed, I procrastinated from writing by researching the age of an old sewing box with the initials SBC for Sarah B. Creller (née White) branded into the hand-carved wood. The Crellers settled in Upstate New York during the colonization of America before the Revolutionary War, and Sarah was my great-great-grandmother on my father's side.

According to family legend—meticulously typed and saved in a three-ring binder—my great-great-grandfather, John, first met Sarah in Union Springs in the Finger Lakes: "He was passing along the street on which she lived one winter in 1869 when he spied a woman's legs sticking out of a snowbank. He pulled the woman out and discovered a charming young lady of nineteen. She had been visiting a neighbor and when running down the path to the street had stubbed her toe on the fence and was thrown forward headfirst into a snowbank. Romance and love followed." They married maybe six months later on July 1, 1869. The sewing box was probably a wedding gift, and it still contains pressed flowers, origin unknown.

Love and romance in winter. *Keep going, it's in your blood,* it whispered to me. I am blessed with a crew of devoted family members, friends, and fans who ensure I keep going with frequents calls, texts, emails, and voices often much louder than a whisper. Many thanks to beta readers Earnie Porta and Barbara Valentin as well as two others who are more like writing coaches. Stacey Porcaro and Heather Anderson ensured I stayed on track with my writing goals to give Katie and Deke their own love story.

Heather Anderson and I had a standing nightly phone call in which she would listen to my day's progress over a glass of chardonnay. (Sometimes more than one glass was necessary!) A fellow woman at the helm, she helped me resurrect her boat, *Char-Don-Eh,* that once plied the Potomac River and was docked one pier over from my boat, the *Princess of*

Tides. Ironically, both of our real vessels enjoyed a short-lived Florida life before going to Neptune's graveyard in Florida's Gulf waters.

Stacey Porcaro was brave (and kind) enough to read my early drafts. Her house was the halfway point between high school and my house when we were growing up, and my walk home from school was often interrupted with a welcome stop for her mother's treats. Although we lost Zelda Wiener in 2023, her potato latkes live on in both memory and her recipe.

When my daughter was young, EmmaLee and I participated in annual ornament exchange parties hosted by my friend and longtime professional confrere Stacey Piper. A couple of those DIY ornaments are hanging on the Christmas tree in Chapter 6. Among my favorite fall harvest recipes is her mother's pumpkin soup. While there are many variations on the recipes in this book, I included ones passed down within my Lamont and Wixson families and my husband's Byrd and McBride families.

I discovered *The American Woman's Cook Book*, edited by Ruth Berolzheimer, when writing this story. It was on my mother's bookshelf, as it may be in your mother's or grandmother's kitchen. First published in 1938 and based on *The Delineator Cook Book*, it was re-released in paperback by Legare Street Press. The history of *The Delineator* magazine is a story in itself. One of the earliest magazines for women, it was founded in 1869 by the Butterick Publishing Company to feature the Butterick sewing patterns. Cookbooks were often given as wedding gifts, and mine was a gift from my father in February 1949: "To my most beloved wife, Marilyn, on our six-month anniversary. Loving you always, Leonard. Honest!! I didn't get this for you because you couldn't cook."

The camaraderie and coaching from writing clubs in the Washington, DC, area and in Florida have been instrumental in the launch of this series. Many thanks to my editor Elizabeth Merck whom I met through my involvement with the Northern Virginia Writers Club. I also owe a debt of gratitude to the Friends of Mason Neck State Park, Potomac River National Wildlife Refuge Complex, and docent Dick Hamly at Pohick Church, for their help in reviewing passages in this novel.

I want to recognize an icon of the Potomac River boating community whose service is sorely missed. Captain Mark Perry ran Rivershore Charters and the ferryboat *Miss Rivershore*. In 2019, they hosted a farewell cruise for my family in which we gave my mother's ashes a final tour of her beloved Belmont Bay. He and his wife Susan shared their love of the region's nature, wildlife, and history on boat tours that ran from Occoquan, until Mark's passing in 2020.

In addition, the river wouldn't be the same for boaters without Tim Bauckman's crab houses. The Dumfries, Virginia, restaurant closed in 2021, and I hope I can do justice to its fun-loving ambience by giving it a fictional rebirth in the Potomac Shores series. You can still sample what will always be my favorite crab cakes on the Potomac at Tim's Rivershore at Fairview Beach in King George. Plus, don't miss the 44 (yes, 44!) frozen concoctions on the menu and the fried snakehead.

The inspiration for the character Danylo and his mural goes to international mural/street artist TakerOne. TakerOne is actually from Hungary, and he stayed at my house when he was painting the mural called "The Fauna of Belmont Bay" on the parking garage of the Potomac Environmental Research and Education Center (PEREC), known as the Potomac Science Center, in fall 2021. Links to TakerOne's website as well as parks and local attractions mentioned in the book can be found in the Resources section of my website at http://www.carolynmcbride.com.

The brightest lights in my life (in no particular order, of course!) are my husband Dennis McBride, my daughter EmmaLee Haga, and now my grandson Onyx Boyne, who came into the world as I finished writing this book. With the addition of another generation to our family, Onyx has profoundly deepened my understanding of love, revealing the boundless capacity of the heart.

HOLIDAY RECIPES

Candy Cane Cookies

Karen Geiger and Susan Kaminsky

COOKIES

1 cup butter	¼ tsp salt
½ cup powdered sugar	2 cups all-purpose flour
1 tsp vanilla extract	¼ tsp baking powder

Cream butter. Add sugar gradually. Blend in vanilla extract, salt, and sifted dry ingredients. Chill. Shape level teaspoonfuls of dough into pencil-thin strips. Turn one end to resemble a cane and place on greased cookie sheets. Bake at 350 degrees for about ten minutes.

PEPPERMINT FROSTING

cream	¼ tsp peppermint extract
1½ cups powdered sugar	Red food coloring
1 tsp vanilla extract	

Add enough cream to powdered sugar to make frosting spreadable. Add extracts. Divide in half, and color one half red. Decorate cookies with alternating strips of red and white.

Makes about two dozen.

Cornbread

Jeanette Byrd

1 cup self-rising cornmeal   1 cup cream corn

1 cup sour cream   2 eggs

½ cup oil

Use enough oil to cover the bottom of a large cast-iron skillet. Put the skillet in the oven to get hot. When oil is heated enough to sizzle, add cornbread mixture and bake at 375 degrees about 30 minutes.

Cranberry-Spiced Martini

Carla Recker

CRANBERRY COMPOTE

1 bag fresh cranberries

1 can crushed pineapple (including juice)

1 cup sugar

1 tsp cardamom

1 tsp cinnamon

½ tsp ground cloves

½ tsp nutmeg

½ tsp salt

Add all compote ingredients to a small saucepan and cook down until thick, approximately 15 to 20 minutes. Once the cranberry mixture is done, cool and store in a refrigerator or freezer, depending on how soon you intend to drink it. It freezes with no issues.

PINEAPPLE ICE CUBES

1 can crushed pineapple (including juice)

Divide second can of crushed pineapple, including juice, equally (about a tablespoon) in 2 mini muffin tins and freeze. Once frozen, remove ice cubes from tins and store in a gallon freezer bag in freezer.

THE MARTINI

3 ounces vodka (or replace with cranberry juice for virgin option)

1 ounce 100-percent cranberry juice

fresh lime juice

Fill shaker full of ice. Pour 2 jiggers (2 ounces) of cranberry compote, 3 jiggers of vodka, and 1 jigger of cranberry juice over ice. Add a splash of lime juice, and shake for 30 to 45 seconds.

RIM GARNISH

½ cup sugar

¼ tsp ground cloves

½ tsp cinnamon

¼ tsp nutmeg

¼ tsp cardamom

Blend sugars and spices in bowl or bag, and then pour into saucer. Wet rim of glass with paper towel, and dip 2 martini glasses into sugar mixture. Add one pineapple ice cube to each glass and fill with shaker ingredients.

Makes 2 martinis. Multiply in equal parts for larger batches.

Green Christmas Wreaths

Elfledia Lamont

⅓ cup butter, melted

32 large marshmallows, melted

1 tsp green food coloring

½ tsp almond extract

½ tsp vanilla

4 cups cornflakes

red cinnamon candies

silver ball candies

Combine all ingredients except candies in large bowl. Shape on wax paper into wreaths while butter and marshmallow are still warm. Allow to set, then decorate with candies.

Icebox Cookies

Elfledia Lamont and Dan Free

1 pound butter

1 cup brown sugar

1 cup granulated sugar

3 eggs

1 tsp baking soda

1 tsp salt

6 cups flour

1 cup finely chopped pecans

Kahlúa for flavor (if desired)

After mixing ingredients, shape on wax paper into rolls 3 to 4 inches long by 1½ inches wide. Refrigerate overnight. Slice into ¼-inch slices of dough and bake at 325 degrees about 12 minutes until firm and light brown.

Makes about 3 dozen cookies.

Pfeffernuss
(pfeffernüsse in German)

Elfledia Plueddemann Lamont

1 cup flour, sifted	1 tsp baking soda
1 tsp cloves	1 tsp anise seed (optional)
1 tbsp cinnamon	1 tsp cardamom seed (optional)
¼ tsp fresh ground black pepper	2 tbsp butter
1 tsp fresh ground nutmeg	2½ cups powdered sugar
½ tsp salt	5 eggs separated

Sift flour, spices, salt, and baking soda. Cream butter and powdered sugar in egg yolks. Mix in dry ingredients. Beat egg whites until stiff and fold into mixture. Chill at least one hour. Roll into strips, cut into nuggets, and shape into balls. Bake on ungreased baking sheets in a 350-degree oven for 15 to 20 minutes. Dust with powdered sugar.

Yields about 9 dozen cookies.

Popcorn Balls

Elfledia Lamont

2 cups granulated sugar

1½ cups water

½ tsp salt

½ cup light corn syrup

1 tsp vinegar

1 tsp vanilla extract

5 quarts popped corn
(we used TV Time)

Butter sides of saucepan. In it, combine sugar, water, salt, syrup, and vinegar. Cook to hard ball stage (250 degrees). Stir in vanilla extract. Slowly pour over popped corn, stirring just to mix well. Butter hands lightly and shape into balls. (We butter the bottom of large bowl containing corn so it won't stick.)

Yields 15–20 balls.

Potato Latkes

Zelda Novick Wiener

1 lb. russet (baking) potatoes, peeled and placed in a bowl of cold water

1 cup grated onion

1 egg, lightly beaten

1 tbsp all-purpose flour or matzo meal

¼ tsp baking powder

½ tsp salt, plus additional salt to taste

freshly ground black pepper to taste

canola or peanut oil, as needed for frying

Line large baking sheet with paper towels. If serving latkes immediately, preheat oven to 200 degrees. Have a large bowl of cold water ready.

Using a hand grater or food processor, grate the potatoes (do not shred). Put grated potatoes in a large colander and squeeze out excess water (a handful at a time) or use a sieve, putting the drained potatoes into a clean bowl. Add onion, eggs, flour, baking powder, salt, and pepper. Mix thoroughly.

Add oil to large skillet (⅛- to ¼-inch) and heat. Spoon 2-3 tablespoons of potato mixture into oil, and press firmly with back of spatula to form thin pancake. Slide latke into hot oil. Do not let latkes touch while frying. Brown on one side (approximately 2 minutes), and then turn and cook until done. Transfer to lined baking sheet to blot excess oil. Add oil as necessary to fry additional latkes.

Keep warm in oven until ready to serve or set aside to cool at room temperature. Refrigerate or freeze. Reheat latkes in 350-degree oven.

Serve with sour cream and/or apple sauce.

Makes about 10 3-inch latkes.

Pumpkin Soup

Suzanne Hohenberg

2½ cups canned pumpkin

¼ cup butter

½ cup finely chopped onion

½ tsp ginger

¼ tsp nutmeg

3½ cups chicken broth

1 cup half-and-half

¼ to ½ cup creamed sherry

salt and pepper to taste

1 tsp brown sugar

Melt butter. Add onion and cook until transparent. Add spices and chicken broth and bring to a boil. Blend in pumpkin. Freeze at this point. Reheat just to a light boil and blend in half-and-half and sherry.

Can be served with a drop of sour cream or chives.

Makes 2 quarts.

Roast Squirrels

The American Woman's Cook Book
(Berolzheimer, 1947)

3 small squirrels

¾ cup salad oil

¼ cup lemon juice
or vinegar

2 cups breadcrumbs

½ cup milk or cream

½ cup diced and
sauteed mushrooms

½ tsp salt

⅛ tsp pepper

½ tsp onion juice

4 tbsp olive oil or bacon fat

1 tsp Worcestershire sauce

paprika

Just kidding! The full recipe is on page 301 of the 1947 edition if you're really interested, but better to fatten them up on birdseed and let them live their lives to antagonize you.

Sunday Sweet Potatoes

Maggie Byrd

3 cups mashed
sweet potatoes

¾ cup sugar

½ cup milk

⅓ cup butter

2 eggs

1 tsp vanilla extract

Combine ingredients and pour into a 9"x13" baking dish.

TOPPING

1 cup coconut

1 cup chopped nuts

1 cup light brown sugar

⅓ cup flour

⅓ cup melted butter

Blend first 4 ingredients. Add butter last. Sprinkle over potatoes. Bake at 375 degrees until brown, about 35 to 40 minutes.

ABOUT THE AUTHOR

CAROLYN McBRIDE is also the author of *The Cicada Spring*, the first novel in the Potomac Shores series. Mother, grandmother, wife, and pet lover, Carolyn writes about the places she lives and loves, from South Florida waters to Virginia's Potomac and Occoquan Rivers, through the eyes of a female boat captain. She is a graduate of the College of William and Mary and former editor and columnist for *National Geographic Traveler*.

To be notified of news releases, please sign up for her newsletter at http://www.carolynmcbride.com or follow her on Facebook at Carolyn McBride – Writer or Instagram via @carolynmcbridewriter.